SHADOWS OVER WOKINGHAM

Chris Robertson

CONTENTS

PROLOGUE: (1998)

Within the claustrophobic confines of the Ship Inn—a decrepit Tudor relic clinging to Wokingham's fading history—young police constable James Thornton finds himself ensnared in a web of unspoken tensions. The pub's nicotine-stained walls pulse with the collective anxiety of its patrons, each clutching their drink as though it were an antidote to some unnameable poison.

Behind the scarred bar, Dave Thompson moves with a precision that belies the storm raging within. His every step echoes the silent fury of a fighter, his rugby-hardened body navigating the cramped space despite the ghost of an old knee injury that flares warnings on these damp nights. As he polishes brass fixtures that gleam unnaturally under the sparse, harsh lights, each deliberate gesture becomes a ritual of defiance—a quiet struggle against the decay of both the building and his own inner turmoil.

Near this battered counter, constable James cradles a pint, his gaze scanning the restless Friday crowd with measured vigilance. At merely twenty-three, he wears the burden of duty like a second skin, his watchful eyes betraying the scars of a soul forced to confront darkness night after night. Then, as if emerging from a fog, his attention falls upon a singular presence radiating both light and an undeniable shadow.

Sarah Matthews, a teacher from The Holt School, sits among her friends and yet seems to stand apart. Fingers tracing nervous patterns on a scratched tabletop, she exudes a fragile brightness that belies the deep fissures of lingering worry. Her laughter, sincere and soft in its Yorkshire lilt, momentarily dispels the heaviness of the room—but her tense shoulders and the anxious drumming of her fingers betray silent battles fought behind the facade of calm. The warm glow catching her auburn hair casts her in an almost angelic light, drawing James's eyes into an unintended collision of fate and apprehension.

With a grace that hints at both escape and entrapment, Sarah drifts toward him and takes a seat at the bar. "Hey there," she murmurs, her voice trembling between hope and dread. "Are you keeping watch over us troublemakers, or are you finding solace on your night off?"

A fragile smile flickers over James's face, creasing his eyes like long-held worry finally finding an outlet. "A bit of both," he replies quietly. His words are punctuated by a subtle, knowing wink exchanged with Dave as another pint is poured—a tacit acknowledgment of the shared burdens that linger like ghosts in the dim light.

Yet beneath that gentle banter, James senses the undercurrent of panic beneath her composed exterior. Her tense shoulders and the restless tapping of her fingers betray a hidden dread. Her eyes repeatedly dart toward the door, as if expecting the intrusion of some unseen menace. "Rough week?" he asks, sliding her drink closer with a tone that brooks no avoidance.

The way she grips her glass—knuckles white with inner strife —speaks of a brewing storm. "Is it that obvious?" she whispers, exhaling a heavy sigh laden with unspoken fears. "The Holt keeps me busy, but it's the outreach work that..." Her voice falters, each word hinting at confessions far darker than schoolyard troubles.

In that fleeting moment, as the overhead light stutters and shadows creep across her face, Sarah is transformed—older, more haunted—her features etched by concerns beyond the ordinary. Overcome by a surge of protectiveness and empathy, James leans in. "Have you noticed anything specific?" he asks, voice low and urgent, a plea to unravel the disintegration behind her carefully masked composure.

Her eyes, a fragile blend of vulnerability and simmering determination, barely register before she replies, "Small things… Danny… he's not the same. Once so full of life, now he drifts like a ghost in his own existence." Her confession is swallowed by the ambient murmur, yet every word is loaded with frustration and fear. "He startles at every sudden noise, constantly glancing over his shoulder—as if the darkness itself were hunting him."

As the discordant strains from the jukebox rise into a new, sorrowful tune, James closes the gap between them, his hand finding hers on the rough bar. The cold, trembling contact speaks of shared terror and unspoken commitment. "You don't have to face this alone," he vows softly, his words a protective shield against the encroaching gloom. "Whatever demons Danny hides, whatever it is that unsettles you… I'll be there."

In the murky light, as flecks of distress and resolve dance in her brown eyes, a fleeting shadow skitters past the window, deepening the tension. "Do you really mean that?" she asks, her voice quavering with a fear that stretches beyond the moment.

"I do." His hand tightens gently, affirming the promise. "Protecting people is my duty, but with you…it goes deeper. I care —more than I probably should."

When last call finally rings out, Sarah begins to gather her things, wrapping a threadbare scarf around her neck as if it could ward off the chill of impending nightmares. "I should head out," she murmurs, her smile a bittersweet blend of melancholy and resolve. "Early start tomorrow...extra rehearsals for the play."

As she rises, James offers quietly, "Let me walk you home."

The cold, misty streets are quiet and empty as James walks alongside Sarah, his mind consumed with conflicting thoughts and emotions. He wants to protect her, to keep her safe from whatever darkness she seems to be facing. But at the same time, he knows there are some battles she must fight on her own.

"This is my street," Sarah says softly, breaking the tense silence between them.

James stops walking and turns to face her, concern etched deeply into his features. "Are you sure you'll be okay?" he asks, the weight of responsibility heavy in his voice.

She smiles wearily, but there is a hint of determination laced within it. "I'll be fine," she reassures him. "I'm used to these streets."

With a nod, James watches as she disappears into the shadows of her apartment building. He takes a deep breath before turning and heading back towards the bar.

As he walks through the deserted streets, his mind is still fixated on Sarah. He wonders what could have caused such a strong-willed and vibrant person to become so troubled. And why does he feel such a strong need to protect her?

Lost in thought, James doesn't notice the figure lurking in the shadows.

CHAPTER 1: 'BITTERSWEET SYMPHONY' (1999)

September light oozed over Wokingham's Market Place like a spectral veil, its pallid glow not a benign beginning but the slow awakening of a town steeped in corruption. Here, the very streets and ancient Tudor facades—weathered monuments that masked centuries of festering decay—seemed to breathe a dark secret, as if Wokingham itself were complicit, nurturing every sordid rumor and every hidden transgression. The autumn morning, with its biting, malevolent chill, collided with the deceptive aroma of freshly baked bread from Taylor's and the cloying scent of Mrs. Patel's chrysanthemums, together forming a bittersweet mockery of the rot that lurked beneath the veneer of genteel respectability. Dominating the scene, the Victorian postbox stood like a silent sentinel, its once-imperial red now the dull hue of old blood, its watchful presence a grim reminder of the sins deeply embedded in the cobblestones.

James moved on his beat with a disturbing mechanical precision, each step on those ancient stones resonating like a heartbeat in a corpse. His Thames Valley Police uniform, once a proud emblem of duty, now felt like a suffocating shroud, its weight a constant, accusatory reminder of his own failures and a town's collective guilt. With every ragged breath, he inhaled the palpable decay of a community that had long ceased to care, its very foundation built on secrets and betrayal.

A cluster of sixth form girls from The Holt School drifted past, their navy blazers immaculate amidst an eerie normalcy that seemed so out-of-place now. Their lighthearted chatter, punctuated by excited plans for a Blur concert at Reading Festival, clashed violently with the ominous pulse of the day. One girl— Katie Williams, whose tentative wave tugged at a long-dormant memory from Sarah's drama group—unwittingly unraveled a thread in the tapestry of James's psyche, dredging up the ferocity of Sarah's passion, her light now extinguished.

The sudden, harsh screech of brakes from a Vauxhall Cavalier at the Broad Street roundabout shattered his spiraling thoughts —an intrusive metallic cry that clawed into his mind. In the midst of assisting a stranded Rover Metro, an RAC van's hazard lights pulsed like an ominous mechanical heartbeat against the oppressive morning grey, each flash a stabbing reminder of fate's cruelty. His Motorola MX3000 radio burst into life with the dispatcher's words: "All units, response needed at Holt Lane near The Holt School. Possible fatality reported. Ambulance en route." The message struck him like a thunderclap, each syllable amplifying his inner fracture as if his chest were being hammered by an unseen force.

For a moment, the sound of The Verve's 'Bittersweet Symphony' emanating from a passing Ford Sierra sliced through his reverie, its melancholic strains mocking the deceptive normalcy of the morning. It was a dirge to his sinking hope, a cruel counterpoint to his mounting horror. With adrenaline and despair entwined, James broke into a frantic run down the claustrophobic alleys of

Rose Street, where even the Methodist Church—once a beacon of solace when Sarah laughed about teaching Sunday school—now seemed haunted by lost promises.

Every echoing footfall resonated across decaying brick, reverberating against a town whose very walls whispered of secrets too unspeakable to confront. He felt like he was being pulled deeper into some twisted vortex as he ran towards the school gates. He could hear his own labored breaths and feel sweat trickling down his face, but all he could focus on was reaching Sarah.

Crowds gathered at the school gates like a living, breathing organism—each face a mask of performative grief and voyeuristic morbid curiosity. Among the throng, shock yielded to the sadistic display of police tape flapping in the wind, and the alternation of red and blue emergency lights painted grotesque silhouettes of horror upon stained cobblestones. With trembling determination, James brandished his warrant card, a feeble talisman in the presence of a town that seemed to have its own agenda—a malignant force dictating which secrets were allowed to fester.

Then, amidst that chaotic ballet of disbelief and despair, he saw her: Sarah's body sprawled out on the pavement like a broken doll. Auburn hair spilled across her pale face like a pool of dark wine. Time distorted—its relentless march fragmenting into jagged shards as his vision tunneled into the macabre scene before him.

Sarah lay motionless, her stillness an affront to life. Her face was peaceful, as

James sank to his knees, the overwhelming sight fracturing his mind into agonizing fragments. The faint bruise hidden beneath her collar, the unnatural bend of her arm, and the ghostly clench of her fingers around a cherished notebook etched themselves into his consciousness, each detail a gash that deepened his trauma. The notebook itself, its worn cover a mute testament to her inner life, pulsed with symbolic urgency—an echo of truths she may have tried to reveal. "No," he choked, the word tearing from him as his hand, trembling and desperate, reached out to her icy cheek. "No, please, Sarah..." Her lingering perfume—a light floral scent, a vestige of last night's fleeting solace at the pub—seared into his memory, its sweetness now an acrid reminder of irrevocable loss.

A paramedic's voice sliced through his disintegrating reverie, "Sir. You need to step back. Please." Unable to extricate himself from the surreal tapestry of guilt and grief, James could only murmur that he knew her—she was everything, and now she was utterly gone, taking with her a piece of his soul. Detective Inspector Peter Grant emerged, his weather-beaten face straining to balance professional detachment with quiet sympathy. "Thornton," he ordered with a measured gravity, "step back. You know the protocol." But James, consumed by both personal despair and an unyielding need to reclaim some shred of truth, pleaded his case weakly even as Grant shut him down with tender finality.

The reprimand echoed like a cruel command against the clamor of forensic teams methodically encircling Sarah's still form. Every flash of camera light blazed like a maggot-infested wound, reducing her to mere evidence—a cold relic of a case that now threatened to swallow his sanity. His mind flickered back to memories of just hours before at The Ship Inn, when Sarah's eyes shone with a fire that has now turned desperately into shadows.

A teacher from The Holt, Miss Jenkins, approached with a tremor in her voice. In murmured recollections of a late Tuesday, she recalled Sarah's whispered fears about a mysterious argument, the quiet tension of a dark Rover 800 lingering in the school's periphery—an omen now mirrored in the details gathered. Each fragment of her testimony tethered James further to this infernal mystery, intensifying his spiraling dive into a nightmare where every discarded clue and every overlooked detail was a link in the chain of relentless guilt.

As the morning unfolded, the sun forced its way higher into a sky that seemed indifferent to the suffering below. Officers expanded the cordon, and amidst scattered radio chatter, house-to-house inquiries, and pleas for CCTV footage, the town churned on with a disquieting regularity—as though Wokingham's malevolent heart beat on, feeding off the dark harvest of secrets and sorrow. A tepid cup of tea from the nearby Polka Dot Café remained untouched in his grasp, its warmth barely countering the chill of death that haunted his every thought. His eyes, however, were invariably drawn to that haunting notebook—sealed now in an evidence bag but resonating with every trembling pencil stroke of Sarah's final frantic notes, each word a desperate dare for someone to understand, to hear the silent scream of truth.

By eleven, the grim ballet reached its crescendo as forensic teams gently lifted Sarah's body onto a stretcher, the black bag that contained her now acting as a stark, morbid contrast against the red brick of the school. As the private ambulance whisked her away, a gust of wind scattered her papers, sending them into a frenzied dance across the playground, like fragile leaves caught in an autumn tempest. Grasping one—a handout for her Year 11 drama class studying "An Inspector Calls"—James felt the bitter sting of irony. Another tragedy, another web of guilt and duty awaiting unraveling.

Slipping the paper into his pocket with a reverence bordering on despair, James stood amid a scene where the world continued its absurd routine. The school bell tolled, a stark reminder that life, in its relentless cruelty, marched on. Through the barren Victorian windows, the absence of students only sharpened the spectral isolation of the moment—a community already marked by darkness.

That evening, alone in the solitary confines of his flat above the shops on Peach Street, James finally dared to open Sarah's notebook. The small, leather-bound journal, dismissed by the forensic team as mundane—a mere repository of a teacher's daily minutiae—had, in his eyes, become an eerie talisman, a final testament of her inner strife. Neat handwriting filled the pages with lesson plans, tender observations, and vibrant ideas for a drama production that had once promised hope. Yet the final entries betrayed a frantic cadence, the hurried scratches of a pen under siege:

"Danny missed another community centre session. When he returned, he wouldn't meet my eyes. Something's wrong—worse than before. He says someone's following him but won't say by whom. I must speak to his social worker at Wokingham Borough Council."

"Noticed a car today—a dark Rover 800, tinted windows. Third time this week outside the school. Probably nothing, but..."

The last line halted abruptly, as if the terror had snatched her voice mid-sentence: "I think someone is—"

A buzz from his phone snapped James from his haunted reverie

—a message from Dave, laden with sorrow and futile promises of support. "Heard what happened. Christ, James, I'm so sorry. Sarah was special. If there's anything you need, anything at all... I'm here till closing."

Special. The word rang hollow against the crushing reality. Sarah had been more than special; she was a beacon of light that now lay extinguished, leaving behind only a void filled with questions and the malignant pulse of a town that thrived on silence and secrets. Outside, Wokingham pressed on with a disconcerting indifference. The headlights of a passing Vauxhall Vectra skimmed over his walls like insidious phantoms, and distant laughter spilled from Market Place—a mockery of normalcy by those oblivious to how profoundly the very soul of Wokingham had been tainted.

The strains of 'Bittersweet Symphony' reverberated in his memory, its melancholic notes intertwining with dread and fragile hope. He recalled Sarah's luminous smile, the vibrancy in her eyes when she spoke of defending those who suffered in silence, and the lingering fear when she mentioned Danny's predicament. Now, driven by a promise forged in the dim haze of pub confessions on a long-forgotten Friday night, James resolved that regardless of official orders or the crushing weight of despair, he would uncover the hidden truth—piece by fraught piece.

Closing the notebook with a final, anguished caress upon its worn cover, he sensed her spirit hovering—a silent whisper urging him to begin anew. Tomorrow, he would search for Danny, he would interrogate her colleagues, he would chase every spectral lead until the malevolent secrets of Wokingham bled into the open. This quest lay beyond mere duty; it was an unspoken pledge to reclaim a stolen light from the jaws of a corrupt and indifferent town. Even if it demanded the entirety of his shattered life.

CHAPTER 2: 'DON'T LOOK BACK IN ANGER' (1999)

The dawn invades James's flat like a malignant autopsy, its grey light a sterile probe dissecting the desolation of his being. Rain hammers the windowpanes like a relentless surgeon, each droplet carving away at memories with brutal precision. His body—a disintegrating machine—lies paralyzed, confined to a bed that has evolved from a haven into a cold, clinical slab for observation.

Sarah's notebook sits on the kitchen table like a damning piece of evidence, its pages mapping the prelude to impending annihilation. Her handwriting—trembling strokes of desperate prophecy—portrays Danny not as a mere student but as a living aberration of dread: "Frightened. Something watching. Must protect." Each letter pulses with a sinister intensity, a vector transmitting unspeakable threats.

The flat itself has decayed into a realm of psychological torment. Walls no longer contain space but crush the soul, compressing it into an oppressive labyrinth. Cracks spider through the ceiling like fractured neural pathways, chronicling a profound existential collapse. James moves with the cold precision of a forensic examiner surveying his own internal crime scene, every measured gesture an indictment of his steady deterioration.

The kettle's whistle splits the morgue-like silence—a sound that is less a mechanical alert than a primal, agonizing wail. Tea transforms into a solemn ritual, a liquid tether between fading memory and the ceaseless agony of unresolved trauma. His fingers trace Sarah's frantic notes with the delicacy of a pathologist mapping ravaged tissue.

Something sinister lurks within the spaces between words. A malignant connection, a mechanism of dread that defies immediate comprehension yet vibrates with a malevolent frequency. James senses it—a splinter lodged deep in his consciousness, a hairline fracture in the fabric of reality itself.

Wokingham mutates as he descends to street level. Familiar landmarks twist into monuments of psychological decay. The off-license, the park, the chippy—each place now a necropolis, a forensic relic of his disintegrating identity. Mist swallows the streets like a spectral autopsy, pavement slick with a fluid evocative of freshly spilled despair.

The police station emerges—a brutalist edifice, a mausoleum to institutional rot. Its redbrick facade no longer commands authority but looms as a sepulcher of buried, unspeakable secrets. James approaches like a damned priest entering a defiled sanctuary, each step a dark ritual of transgression.

DI Peter Grant's office is a crypt of bureaucratic silence. Grant himself—stooped and grim like a medieval sentinel— embodies the sterile architecture of a heartless institution. Their conversation morphs into a macabre dance, words wielded with the exactitude of scalpel strokes in a morbid autopsy.

"Truth's got teeth," Grant intones, voice low and foreboding, "and it don't much care who it devours."

The council flats arise from the urban fog like calcified tumors of collective despair. Concrete facades bear the scars of time—water stains blooming like virulent infections, wallpaper peeling to reveal the diseased skeleton of the structure beneath. The eye, carved into plaster, shifts from mere vandalism to an ominous sigil, marking territories conquered by psychological terror.

In Danny's forsaken flat, abandonment has coalesced into a tangible state of decay. Scattered newspapers clatter like desiccated neural transmissions of a mind long dead. The flyer James uncovers—with its stark, unblinking eye—is no mere scrap but a contagion, damning evidence of a systemic corruption seeped in darkness.

"They see everything."

The words etch themselves into his consciousness, a diagnostic revelation that distorts his every perception. James recoils, each step a calculated retreat from a sprawling crime scene that defies the confines of flesh and stone.

His Ford Escort morphs into a mobile coffin of isolation. Oasis's "Wonderwall" crackles through the speakers like a requiem for lost hope, Gallagher's tone a spectral witness to the unraveling catastrophe. The ever-watchful eye stalks him from every shadow, every fleeting glimpse a reminder of inescapable doom.

Truth awaits—a predatory mechanism entangled in the very fabric of Wokingham's bleak existence.

And James, driven by a relentless hunger for revelation, will pursue it—even if the path leads further into the abyss of his own unraveling soul.

CHAPTER 3:
'WONDERWALL' (1999)

The rain was no benign cascade but a horde of invasive parasites, saturating James with every lethal droplet—each carrying a fragment of Sarah's unbearable absence. It clawed at him, seeping into his marrow with a malevolent persistence that echoed the drumming terror in his skull. Sleep had become a cruel specter, shattered by not just memory but vivid hallucinations: Sarah's blank, unfeeling eyes and Danny's quivering whispers, their voices merging with nameless, looming threats that prowled just out of focus. Even his flat, once a refuge, had turned into a sentient beast; its walls heaved with malignant respiration, expanding and contracting as if alive, pulsing with the arrhythmic heartbeat of repressed nightmares.

At dawn, when a pallid light bled through the curtains like an open wound, James lay frozen in his bed. His eyes traced the ever-changing spiderweb of cracks on the ceiling, each fissure a prophecy of collapse and decay. His body throbbed with exhaustion, heavy and toxic, weighed down by guilt that gnawed at him relentlessly. The flat's once comforting confines now exhaled a suffocating miasma; every corner birthed shadows that shuddered and breathed with a sinister life of their own.

Sarah's battered notebook lay on the kitchen table like an accusatory relic. Its wrinkled pages bore frantic scrawls—a desperate confession: "Danny—so worried. He's frightened. I need to help him." The words coiled around his heart like vicious barbed wire, merging grief with a savage, protectiveness that feasted upon his sanity until the distinction between emotion and obsession blurred into a single, overwhelming torment.

A sudden, shrill whistle from the aging kettle tore through a silence that felt as if the very walls were whispering secrets of despair. As James prepared his tea in a trance, his hands moved mechanically, detached from the turbulent storm inside his mind. The scorching liquid seared his throat, yet the pain was drowned out by the clamor of his internal demons.

Between the frantic lines of Sarah's frantic scribbles, something insidious hid in the margins—a truth so potent that it had written her death. It was an errant shard of reality embedded beneath his skin, festering into poison, making every darkened corner of the flat brim with malignant intent.

With a heavy jacket cloaking him like a shroud, James descended the narrow, creaking stairs. Outside, Wokingham was suffocating beneath a murky veil of mist, its pavement not merely wet but slick with the sheen of fresh, dark blood. The town itself seemed to conspire against him, twisting into leering, monstrous forms that mocked his suffering.

Driving his sputtering Ford Escort toward St. Crispin's School, the vehicle coughed against the cold, damp air. The school, a brooding monument of Victorian decay, loomed with secrets buried beneath its timeworn facade. Inside, the hallways became a labyrinth echoing with his lone, haunted footsteps, every sound amplified by a pre-dawn emptiness that pulsed with anticipation.

In Sarah's abandoned classroom—a mausoleum of unfinished

lessons—the remnants of a life abruptly halted lay scattered: half-marked essays, dust gathering on forgotten drama props, and her coffee mug deserted on the desk, a silent witness longing for her return. Like a specter, James roamed these desolate relics of the past; the dust motes in the stale light seemed to churn with memories of what was lost, as if the room itself was mourning.

A stubborn drawer yielded a jumble of teaching supplies and hidden horrors until beneath a disorganized stack of worksheets, he unearthed a small, black diary that pulsed with dread. Unlike the pragmatic pages of her notebook, these pages were inscribed with a desperate urgency, the ink pressed deeply in a manner that threatened to tear the paper apart. "Car following me again. Dark Rover 800. Can't see the driver but I know they're watching. Always watching. Danny says they have eyes everywhere. I didn't understand at first, but now…" Each word hammered into him, confirming that Sarah hadn't been the paranoid one—she'd been prey.

As the diary trembled in his grasp, a memory surged forth: Sarah at The Ship Inn, her fragile fingers trembling around a glass as she whispered of Danny with a terror so palpable it had slithered through the air like poison. Even then, her voice trembled with foreboding, but James had been too ensnared by the comfortable illusion of normality that cloaked Wokingham in genteel deceit.

A noise in the corridor sent his pulse into overdrive—a sound as ominous as the sighing of an ancient beast. Yet, it was only the radiator groaning, its pipes lamenting like a chorus of tortured souls. With the diary pressed against his chest, James felt its weight as a grim reminder of his failure.

The drive to Remington Road transformed into a descent into a Victorian nightmare. The council flats rose from the swirling mist like decaying monoliths, their concrete faces marred by relentless urban decay. Every window stared dead-eyed at a world forsaken by hope. Danny's flat, perched on the fifth floor of a crumbling building with a perpetually broken elevator, forced James into a climb through corridors reeking of neglect and despair. The dimly lit passage stretched before him like the gullet of some monstrous creature, fluorescent lights flickering overhead like the erratic heartbeat of a dying giant. Amid the graffiti—savage, primal scribbles—one symbol recurred with a sinister insistence: an ever-watching eye.

The door to Danny's flat hung ajar, its splintered frame bearing the fresh scars of violence. Instinctively, James reached for his service weapon—and found only empty space. With a push of his shoulder, the door creaked open in protest, revealing a scene of disarray: drawers flung wide, scattered belongings drenched in the residue of hurried flight, and a half-eaten meal congealing into the grim tapestry of abandoned hope. Yet it was the walls that ensnared his gaze—they were covered in a chaotic multitude of drawings, overlapping feverish impressions of eyes that followed him relentlessly, some crudely drawn, others rendered with unnerving precision, as if the very room were alive and intent on consuming him.

On a ragged scrap of wallpaper, Danny's shaking scrawl proclaimed, "They see everything. They know everything. They're coming for me like they came for her."

The sight stole his breath. In a dim corner, beneath an overturned chair, the jagged shape of Sarah's phone emerged—the very one that had vanished from the crime scene. Its cracked screen flickered weakly to life as he pressed the power button, and one unread message glared at him like a death sentence: "I know what they're doing at the estate. I have proof. Meet me at midnight. Tell no one." The message came from a number James knew well—a number belonging to an ally, a confidant Sarah had trusted. Each revelation stung like a shard, etching another cut into his already shattered psyche.

A soft scuffle behind him made him whirl around; the hallway appeared desolate, yet the oppressive atmosphere shifted palpably —as if the very air had thickened with malevolent intelligence. Then, like a malignant caption scrawled by fate, red ink still wet on the wall declared: "YOU'RE NEXT." The eyes in the drawings seemed to converge upon him, predatory and unyielding, as the walls themselves pulsed with the threat of impending doom.

Clutching Sarah's phone, his palms slick with nervous sweat, James staggered toward the door. He had found more than he sought, and now he had to survive the wrath of the living nightmare that had been unleashed. Every step back through the corridor felt interminable, the passage twisting like a dark vein beneath the skin of the building. At the stairwell, a shadow slid along the edge of his vision—a whisper of movement, the susurration of fabric against concrete. Driven by raw, unadulterated fear, he sprinted down the stairs, each stride a desperate bid to outrun a fate already written.

Emerging into the feeble light of day, James gulped in air tainted with diesel and decay. His car awaited him, but it too was a part of the conspiracy: the windshield bore the mark of that relentless, accusing eye, drawn in condensation as though nature itself had taken up arms against him.

The engine roared to a reluctant life as he turned the key, the ancient stereo blasting Liam Gallagher's sneering anthem—an ironic soundtrack to his crisis. Tires squealed, and as he pulled away, a dark shape emerged from the building's entrance, a silent sentinel watching his retreat with predatory patience.

The truth fermented within him—a cancer, a relentless entity feeding on his every thought. The conspiracy was a labyrinth far deeper and more pungent than he had ever anticipated; somewhere amidst the relentless surveillance and whispered threats, Danny carried the incriminating secret that had bled Sarah onto cold pavement. He pressed harder on the accelerator, fleeing through streets that had transformed into a diseased carnival of decay. The once-charming Tudor facades now bore the gaping wounds of cruelty, their timber bones exposed like the ribs of a long-dead carcass. The unyielding drizzle was no mere rain— it was a cascade of grimy, tearful judgment washing over the town as if the skies lamented its corruption.

In his mind, the message on Sarah's phone echoed relentlessly, a splintering chorus that pricked his soul with every thought. Some trusted ally had sent it—a piercing beacon meant to disrupt the sinister order that had turned this quaint market town into a panopticon of lurking eyes and whispered threats.

The Ship Inn loomed ahead, a deceptive sanctuary glowing with warm, inviting light that masked poison beneath its polished veneer. Parking in its cramped lot, James killed the engine but remained trapped behind the wheel as he contemplated the grim figures within. Through the pub's windows, where light spilled like a false promise onto slick cobblestones, he knew Dave was there—polishing glasses with mechanical detachment, unknowingly witnessing the town's slow, agonizing rot.

The weight of Sarah's phone in his pocket was tangible, a constant reminder of a message laden with malevolent possibility: "I know what they're doing at the estate." What unspeakable truths had she uncovered in those decaying records? What corruption was so deep that it had signed her death warrant?

The pub door creaked open under the strain of ancient wood surrendering to inevitable decay. Inside, the scents of stale ale and chemical polish had soured, now reeked of desperate secrets. Dave looked up behind the bar, his lined face etched with a sorrow that mirrored the gloom in the air.

"Christ, mate," Dave murmured, reaching for a glass. "You look like you've seen a ghost."

"Maybe I have," James rasped, his voice raw with the anguish of haunted memories. "The past in this town... it never dies, does it, Dave?"

Dave's hands stilled, his eyes flickering with the terror of buried truths. "No, it doesn't. But some things... some things should remain entombed for everyone's sake."

Those words were a dire warning. As James leaned over the scarred bar top, his whisper was weighted with secrets and confessions, "They're watching me, Dave. I'm marked—just like her, just like Danny. Soon, the truth will claw its way out, and it won't matter who lets it."

Dave's hands trembled as he poured a double whiskey, the amber liquid writhing like captured blood; "It was meant to be simple, James. The estate... it was supposed to be clean, but then the questions began, and people started to vanish."

The untouched glass between them reflected the pub's sorrowful lights, fractured and ominous. James could sense invisible eyes, a relentless scrutiny leaching the very warmth from the timbers overhead.

"They used this place, didn't they?" The realization struck him like frost on living skin. "The Ship Inn—a respectable guise to hide monstrous dealings while the town slumbered."

Dave's expression crumpled, decades of despair etched into every line of his face. "You have no idea what they're capable of—the reach they have, the measures they take to silence dissent." He glanced fearfully at the rain-traced windows, where the droplets wept like dark omens. "Sarah... she discovered something in those records. Something that stretched from our backwater estate to the corridors of power in London."

The name hung between them like a noose, the phone in James's pocket a bleeding reminder of that night's message. "Her message wasn't just a meeting invitation, was it? It was a trap."

"They knew she'd come," Dave whispered, horror and sorrow mingling in his voice. "They knew she'd risk everything to expose them. To save Danny. And now..." His words died as the pub door creaked open once more.

A figure, outlined against the rain, entered—a man with an expensive overcoat dripping with water. The scar on his cheek glistened like a fresh wound as he smiled with a predatory grace.

"Detective Thornton," he said, his cultured tone laced with unyielding menace. "I believe we need to discuss boundaries. When it becomes necessary to let sleeping dogs lie."

The very air in the pub thickened as though charged with impending violence, each breath a struggle against the oppressive force closing in. In that suffocating moment, James felt the malignancy of the truth harden in his bones—it was too late to escape. The darkness that had claimed Sarah now reached out, patient and relentless, its tendrils ready to ensnare him too.

Somewhere in the rain-soaked labyrinth of Wokingham, Danny was still out there, clutching the secret that had cost Sarah her life. The scarred man's Oxford shoes clicked ominously on the worn floorboards as he advanced, each step compressing the room's air until every breath felt like a battle for survival. The rain, streaking his lavish coat in oily trails that stained the floor like pooling blood, bore silent witness to the unfolding catastrophe.

"You've been persistent, Detective," the man murmured, his voice as cultured as it was cold. "Persistence without wisdom... that's little more than suicide, wouldn't you agree?"

James tensed, every fiber of his being coiled with the threat of violence. Behind him, Dave's breath became shallow as though he too sensed the specter of doom. The amber of the whiskey fractured under lost light like dying stars, each reflection a grim warning.

"Sarah wasn't persistent enough for you?" James growled, his voice a low, seething thunder of repressed fury. "Or was she too persistent? She uncovered something in those estate records—something you'd rather bury with all the inconvenient truths."

The scarred man's expression remained inscrutable, though a predator's gleam danced in his eyes. "Miss Matthews made her choices," he said softly, each word a precise incision. "And now, Detective, the question is whether you're ready to follow her down the same treacherous path."

The threat hung heavy, a toxic miasma that seeped into every shadow of the ancient pub. James felt the oppressive weight of history crushing him—the many lives ruined by secrets exchanged over drinks, the countless deals struck in whispers beneath such very beams.

"The boy knows, doesn't he?" James pressed, desperation edging his tone. "Danny saw something at the estate, something those in power would kill to keep hidden."

A fleeting flash of emotion—a hint of concern perhaps—flickered across the scarred man's face before vanishing behind a veneer of contempt. "Children wield imaginations as fierce as any conspiracy theory," he replied coolly. "They see monsters in every shadow—much like grieving detectives, wouldn't you say?"

He stepped closer, his expensive cologne mingling with the stench of decay, too refined to hide the rot beneath. "Consider this a professional courtesy, Detective. A final chance to step back before the abyss swallows you whole. After all..." His smile broadened, the scar on his cheek a grotesque emblem. "We wouldn't want another tragedy—to add to the long list in our once-lovely town."

James's pulse thundered as he saw Dave tense behind the bar, an unspoken warning amid the dread. The scarred man's predatory gaze shifted momentarily, then locked back onto James.

"Think it over," he commanded, already moving toward the door. "But not here. The countryside can be... treacherous. Accidents, they happen." His hand lingered on the doorknob as if savoring the threat. "And Miss Matthews... she never saw it coming. She thought she could change things."

With a creak and slam, the door closed, leaving the space trapped in a silence weighted by unspeakable threats. Dave's shaking hands emerged once more as he whispered, "Oh God, James... what have you done?"

But James was ensnared in his thoughts, fragments of dark secrets clashing like shards of broken glass in his mind. The oppressive sensation of being watched—a malignant, all-consuming eye—haunted him relentlessly. Outside, rain battered the town with a venomous fury, a deluge that seemed to carry the very essence of loss. Somewhere within that storm, Danny roamed—a living vessel of the dangerous truth that had claimed Sarah.

Time was slipping away. Each beat of his racing heart was a countdown to a destiny intertwined with betrayal and horror. As James gripped the steering wheel, knuckles bleached white by agonizing intensity, the familiar streets of Wokingham transformed into a nocturnal labyrinth of decay. Tudor facades, once symbols of quaint charm, now appeared as grim, accusing specters—exposed bones in the carcass of the town. The persistent, invasive drizzle was no mere weather pattern; it was a relentless, living presence, weeping grimy tears into every crack and crevice.

The message on Sarah's phone gnawed at him, each word a poisonous splinter deeper than the last. Lost in relentless thought, he navigated toward The Ship Inn—a façade of warmth that now seemed a hollow trap. Parking in the cramped lot, he sat in the cold engine, the memory of Sarah's urgent words thrumming in his ear. Inside that pub, under deceptive lights and the clink of glasses, Dave was bound to be there, an unwitting chronicler of the degeneration that had consumed their town.

The door of the pub creaked and swung open, echoing the decay of ancient wood. Inside, the air was thick with artificially sweet aromas and the sour tang of stale ale. Dave, his eyes wide with a silent plea, met James's haunted stare.

"Christ, mate," Dave uttered slowly. "You look as if you've been devoured by the past."

"Perhaps I have," James rasped, voice raw with despair. "The past—this town's darkness—refuses to die. It festers like a living wound. Who was it that sealed her fate, Dave? Who sent her to her death?"

Dave's face paled, and his trembling hands betrayed his unspoken terror. "Don't... Some questions, James, once answered, unlock horrors that can never be contained. They are doors that, once open, become our tomb."

Leaning over the battered bar, James's whisper was laden with the raw intensity of inner decay. "They're watching me, Dave. I'm marked now—just as she was, just as Danny is. The truth will emerge, no matter the cost."

Dave's hands faltered as he poured a double of whiskey—a dark, glistening liquid that moved with the slow inevitability of blood. "It wasn't meant to go so far," he murmured, eyes glassy with regret. "The estate... once a symbol of order, it morphed into a labyrinth of corruption when inquisitive souls began to pry. And then people vanished."

The untouched whiskey mirrored the breaking light, like shattered reflections of a dying star. James could almost sense the invisible, probing eyes lurking in the pub's cold corners, the very beams overhead seeming to pulse with sinister intent.

"They used this establishment, didn't they?" James finally pressed. "The Ship Inn—presenting itself as respectable, while beneath it lay a den of clandestine cruelty."

Dave's sorrow deepened into despair. "You have no idea," he replied in a hushed, urgent tone. "They are powerful—darker forces with tendrils reaching far beyond this town. Sarah unearthed something in those records—a secret so monstrous it went all the way to London, perhaps higher."

The weight of that revelation pressed upon James as his fingertips brushed against the cracked screen of Sarah's phone. "That message... it wasn't merely an invitation. It was a signal that she had fallen into a trap."

"They knew she couldn't resist," Dave said, voice hushed and haunted. "They knew she had to expose them. And now the game has turned on us all."

Just then, the pub's door creaked open again. A silhouette materialized beneath the pallid light—a man whose expensive overcoat was drenched in rain, droplets streaking his coat like oily tears. The scar on his cheek shone malevolently as he regarded them with a chilling smile.

"Detective Thornton," he intoned, voice smooth and deadly. "We need to talk about boundaries. About knowing when to let the past lie undisturbed."

In that moment, the very atmosphere thickened, the ambient air seeming to conspire with the man's threat, exerting a pressure that made each breath a struggle. James felt the malignant force crystallize within him—there was no escape from this swirling vortex of corruption. The darkness in Wokingham had decided its next victim.

And somewhere out there, amid the eternal rain, Danny lingered with the secret that had damned Sarah—a secret worth every drop of blood spilled. The scarred man's measured steps echoed like ominous countdowns as he advanced, while rain ran down his coat, staining the worn floor in patterns reminiscent of pooling, dark blood.

"You've been persistent, Detective," the man rasped, his tone a cruel blend of cultured menace and sinister decay. "Persistence without wisdom is nothing but suicide."

James's every muscle locked with the imminent threat. Dave's silent terror behind the bar was almost tangible, the fractured light dancing on the whiskey as if heralding impending doom.

"Was Sarah not persistent enough for you?" James snarled, his voice a guttural growl of despair and fury. "Or was she too persistent? She uncovered truths in the estate records that you'd prefer to hide beneath layers of polished lies."

The scarred man's eyes flickered a predator's cold, calculated interest. "Miss Matthews made poor choices," he said softly, each syllable a scalpel's incision into the air. "Now, Detective, the question is whether you will follow in her doomed footsteps."

His words were toxic, permeating every dark recess of the room, dragging the ghosts of the past into the present. James felt the crushing weight of their implications—countless lives reduced to hushed secrets and violent silences.

"The boy—Danny—he must know, shouldn't he?" James pleaded, desperation overtaking him. "He glimpsed something at the estate that wasn't meant for mortal eyes."

A shadow of concern flashed briefly over the scarred man's visage before vanishing beneath an icy veneer. "Children's minds weave tales of monsters and conspiracies," he replied coolly. "Much like grieving detectives who concoct their vendettas in trembling whispers."

He drew nearer, his cologne a cloying mix of elegance and decay that did nothing to mask his corruption. "Consider this a courtesy, Detective—a chance to step back before you are swallowed whole by the abyss. After all…" His smile widened, the scar on his cheek a grotesque reminder, "we wouldn't want another tragedy in this so-called town. Not when we're still mourning the last one."

The gravity of his words slammed into James, his heart pounding a frantic rhythm as he saw Dave tense in silent terror behind the bar. The man's predatory gaze fixed on James, finality in its cold calculation.

"Think about it," he said, already striding toward the exit. "But not here. Out in the countryside, the terrain becomes treacherous —accidents, unforeseen as they are inevitable." His hand rested momentarily on the door, as if savoring the threat. "Miss Matthews never saw it coming. She believed she could make a difference."

With a resounding slam, the door closed, leaving behind a suffocating silence thick with unspoken menace. Dave's trembling hands emerged once more, his voice a broken whisper, "Oh God, James... what have you done?"

But James was lost in a mire of shattered fragments and malignant revelations—the pieces of a conspiracy too vast to escape. The ancient walls, alive with pulsing, malignant memories, closed in around him, each heartbeat a drum signaling imminent doom. Outside, the unending rain, a poisonous deluge, veiled the town in sorrow and judgment. And lurking within that storm was Danny, the reluctant bearer of a secret far darker than the countless tragedies that had already claimed their lives.

Time was eroding fast, and as James gripped the steering wheel with desperate fury, Wokingham's once-familiar streets transformed into a nightmarish maze of corrupted beauty— a town whose very architecture had become an antagonist, its Tudor facades now grim specters of mortality. The oppressive rain continued its relentless assault, an invasive force that dripped into his soul like cursed blood, and each drop bore the everlasting echo of Sarah's absence.

There was no turning back now—the malignant past, the grotesque present, and the uncertain future converged into one living nightmare, where every step forward was a descent deeper into the monstrous heart of corruption.

CHAPTER 4:
'PARKLIFE' (2023)

The grey light of dawn did not merely crawl but erupted across Elms Field like a metastasizing malignancy, corrupting the revitalized park into an anatomical aberration. The scruffy wasteland of James's memory had vanished, supplanted by an artificially manicured facade that sneered at the decay festering beneath its surface. The new playground equipment loomed like instruments of clinical torture against a sky congested with the town's suppressed secrets, while the benches lurked as predatory parasites—waiting to extract every morsel of psychological sustenance from any unsuspecting victim. Even the café, with its garish parasols and frenetic morning bustle, served only as a flimsy veneer over decades of accumulated darkness.

James stood at the field's edge, his eyes absorbing the manufactured normality with a churn of revulsion and despair. The weight of twenty-five years pressed down upon him like cemetery dirt, each breath a struggle against the suffocating burden of memory and guilt. Somewhere in the distance, the muffled strains of "Parklife" seeped from a portable speaker, the once jubilant melody now perverted into something sinister and derisive.

Then, like a violent neurological event firing across a darkened cortex, Miss Jenkins materialized from the morning mist. Her sudden emergence—oversized sunglasses failing to mask the haunted hollows of her eyes—was nothing short of seismic. Time and grief had carved deep channels into her face, transforming what were once laugh lines into topographical maps of sorrow, and as she shrank into herself, she seemed determined to vanish in the presence of the malevolent forces still lurking in the shadows.

"Detective Thornton," she greeted, her voice brittle and on the verge of shattering in the chill air. Her hands engaged in an anxious dance on her lap—fingers knotting and unknotting like pale, restless spiders.

"Just James, please," he replied, easing himself onto a bench whose damp wood seeped coldness through his clothes like the caress of a dead hand. He maintained a guarded distance, recognizing in her the same skittish, wounded air as that of a beleaguered animal.

They sat in an uneasy silence, watching parents shepherd their children through their morning routines with blissful ignorance of the darkness that had once claimed this space. How many among them knew of Sarah? Of the conspiracy that had choked the life from her and left its poisonous tendrils spiraling around the heart of Wokingham?

"I found something," Miss Jenkins finally whispered, her voice barely disturbing the stagnant air. With trembling fingers that treated the item like an unexploded bomb, she retrieved a folded piece of paper from her bag. "In Sarah's things. I should have given it to you years ago... but I was afraid. God, I was so afraid."

The paper trembled between them as if it were alive. James accepted it gently, his heart pounding as he unfolded the yellowed sheet. Before him lay a list of names, the ink faded yet stubbornly legible. His breath hitched when he spotted Danny's name midway, alongside Sarah's hurried annotation: "They're watching." Below that, scratched in frantic, jagged strokes, was the crude outline of an eye—its dilated pupil exuding a malevolence he recognized all too well. It was the same symbol he'd seen carved into rotting doorframes and jeering on crumbling walls, a silent sentinel staking territory for something vast and corrupt.

James's grip on the paper tightened until his knuckles turned white, with each name seared into his consciousness like a burning brand. The eye seemed to pulse with its own malignant awareness, a sentient observer that taunted him through the yellowed page. His mind recoiled back to the decaying council estates where he'd first encountered it—carved with obsessive precision as if marking an empire claimed by unspeakable corruption.

"Where did you find this?" he rasped, his voice scraping against the morning air like rust on old metal.

Miss Jenkins flinched at the sound, her shoulders hunching in anticipation of an unseen blow. "Her classroom," she managed in a hushed tone, her eyes darting around the park like a trapped animal. "The day after we lost her. It was tucked away in her desk drawer amid a stack of unmarked essays. I didn't know what to make of it then, but it felt important—like a fragment of her I could hold onto."

Fresh tears welled in her red-rimmed eyes, spilling down cheeks etched by decades of grief. "I'm so sorry, James. I should've spoken up sooner. I should have been braver."

"No," James interjected more harshly than intended before softening his tone, reaching out to steady her trembling arm. "No, you did the right thing by keeping it safe. This is a thread—a breadcrumb drawing us closer to the truth."

Her gaze locked with his in desperate intensity. "You have to be careful, James," she pleaded. "Whatever Sarah uncovered...I believe it's still out there. Still watching. Waiting."

The words sent a chill coursing through him. He recalled the strange, unmarked cars now frequenting outside his flat; the muffled footsteps stalking him along Wokingham's twisted streets; the oppressive sensation of unseen eyes pinning him in place, patient as a spider weaving its web.

"I know," he murmured quietly, meeting her haunted gaze. "But I can't stop now—not when I'm this close. I owe her that much."

Miss Jenkins held his eyes a moment longer—a silent benediction wrapped in both warning and grief—before nodding once. James then stood and tucked the precious paper into his coat pocket like a talisman, surveying Elms Field one last time. He took in the oblivious families and laughing children, the meticulously maintained illusion of normalcy that barely concealed the cancer of corruption rotting beneath. The playground equipment threw elongated, merciless shadows across manicured grass like the bars of a vast, inescapable cage, while the morning mist seeped in like poisonous vapor, carrying whispers of century-old secrets. Even the trees loomed with predatory intent, their gnarled branches reaching as if to ensnare any who dared look too deeply.

Everything about this place reeked of decay—a modern mask

over a corpse, a cosmetic cover-up for the festering rot beneath Wokingham's genteel surface. In that hidden decay, woven into a complex web of lies and surveillance, lay the truth about Sarah's death.

"Not this time," James vowed silently, his jaw locking against the surge of rage and grief rising within him. "Not again."

He strode away from the park bench, leaving Miss Jenkins and the ghosts of happier days behind. The phantom strains of "Parklife" faded into the distance, overtaken by the pounding of his own heartbeat and the soft whisper of gathering storm clouds. He clutched his new lead—a fragile, elusive thread—and prepared to unravel the puzzle, one connection at a time.

The oppressive clouds descended as he approached his car, their weight matching the crushing burden of revelation lodged in his chest. The list of names seared against his heart, reopening wounds long thought healed. The morning had taken on a fevered quality, its reality bending at the edges like shimmering heat waves over scorched pavement.

His Ford Escort crouched at the curb like a dormant beast, its rusted body adorned with beads of moisture that resembled weeping tears—or perhaps silent blood. James's hands trembled as he unlocked the door, the key scraping against the metal with a sound reminiscent of distant, anguished screams. Inside, the confined space of the car felt oppressive, steeped in decades of accumulated grief and impotent rage. The steering wheel was icy beneath his palms—the worn leather attesting to countless moments of white-knuckled determination during devastating hours like these.

Before starting the engine, he lingered, his gaze drifting back to Elms Field through the windscreen. The park's meticulously preserved façade shimmered and distorted, its modern amenities impotent against the corruption seeping from deep within the earth. Miss Jenkins remained alone on the bench, a diminished, fragile figure slowly consumed by the rising mist—a testament to the secrets she bore. The sight twisted his gut into knots. How many others like her lurked in plain sight, clutching shards of puzzles that had cost Sarah her life?

The jagged eye symbol from his investigation flashed before him, its erratic lines shifting as though it were staring right back with malignant intent. The sensation of being watched was relentless now—mirrored in shop windows, caught on security feeds, and lurking in the inky shadows where light dared not intrude. That constant scrutiny had become as familiar as his own heartbeat.

A sudden movement in his rearview mirror snapped his attention —a dark vehicle slipping past smoothly, its windows tinted like a predator's mask. His heart pounded as a vaguely familiar face appeared in the fleeting reflection before the car melted into the thickening fog.

The message was clear. They knew he was getting too close. The same forces that had stalked Sarah in her final days now closed in on him, waiting with the patience of vultures poised to strike.

James's grip on the steering wheel tightened until his knuckles blanched white. Let them come, he thought. He now had leads —fragile pieces of a vast puzzle woven by corruption that had claimed Sarah's life. He would follow every thread, tear down every wall of deceit until the raw, unflinching truth lay exposed in the harsh light of day.

Starting the engine, he drove away from Elms Field and its carefully constructed façade. Wokingham unfurled before him like a gaping wound, its once-familiar streets now infused with peril. Amid this labyrinth of Victorian structures and Tudor façades, the answers he craved lay hidden, and he would find them —even if it meant burning his own town to ashes.

Sarah's voice echoed faintly from the passenger seat, both comforting and taunting—a ghostly reminder that her spirit was with him in his crusade for justice. He could almost catch a lingering trace of her delicate, floral perfume, a scent that had haunted him for twenty-five long years.

The roaring engine of the Escort resounded like an enraged beast as James slammed his foot on the accelerator, determined to carve a path deep into the heart of the darkness that had devoured Wokingham. The truth lay somewhere in that morass, waiting to be uncovered. And this time, James Thornton was ready to confront whatever horrors it might unleash.

Yet as he drove further into the unknown, a mingling of fear and determination churned within him. Was he truly prepared for the gruesome, twisted revelations that awaited? Only time would tell.

CHAPTER 5: 'THE DRUGS DON'T WORK' (1999)

Rain wasn't just falling; it was a vengeful curse, each drop slashing at James's skin and soul as he drove through Wokingham's twilight—a city that seemed to conspire against him. The sodium-lit streets warped into corridors of liquid shadow, where every glistening rivulet felt like a whispered indictment. Guiding the Escort along twisted, unrecognizable routes that morphed familiar roads into gaunt cycles of dread, each turn drew him inexorably closer to the Remington Road estate. The windshield wipers moved in a relentless, metronomic judgment, their sweep measuring out the seconds until he confronted the boy whose name—Danny—had been murmured in Sarah's laments like a benediction against corruption.

Through the curtain of murderous rain, the estate loomed— a dystopian assembly of brutalist towers rising like decrepit monoliths from a wasteland. The concrete walls were a canvas for decay, overtaken with graffiti that slithered like dark secrets, and that ominous eye symbol repeated over and over, its unblinking stare following every hesitant step. James killed the engine beneath a gaunt oak whose twisted, claw-like branches scratched at a black sky swollen with further promises of retribution.

Sixty yards off, Danny was crumpled on a rain-soaked bench, his small body contorted by belied terror. His trembling limbs and the frantic way his eyes darted through the darkness painted a vivid picture of a child physically betrayed by an unyielding horror. Even from this distance, James could see the desperate tension etched into the boy's stiff posture, as if every shudder was an unspoken scream. The rain, cold and accusatory, mingled with Danny's sweat, accentuating the terror that was far too large for him—a terror that had cost Sarah her life.

"Danny." The word floated out in a quiet, tentative murmur that struggled against the angry roar of the storm. The boy's head jerked up, his feral, wide eyes searing into James—the same haunted depths that had belonged to Sarah. In that instant, it was as if a predator had already claimed him, leaving a scar none could see.

"Told you not to come here," Danny managed in a near-whisper, his voice broken as his gaze flitted to the encroaching shadows. "They... they see everything. Every damn thing." His fingers twisted into anxious scrapes against the frayed cuff of his sleeve, his knuckles white with genuine terror.

James eased himself onto the bench's far end, giving the boy just enough room to vanish into the storm's maw if need be. The icy water seeped through his trousers, a chill as unwelcome as the grave. "Tell me about the men who watch," he said, his tone as soft and grave as the falling rain. "The ones Sarah was hunting."

Danny's voice trembled like a broken record, a rapid torrent of fearful details as he recounted his observations. "Black cars. Shiny, expensive ones. They prowl around the estate at night, circling like death's vultures waiting for their prey." With trembling urgency, his small hand brushed a jagged scar down his cheek—a gruesome memento etched on his skin—and his eyes shone with raw horror. "I saw one near Miss Matthews outside The Ship, and she…she was crying. I'd never seen her cry before."

A shock of ice slid through James's veins as every unsettling piece merged into a portrait of malevolence. That scarred man —known only through furtive glances—had stalked Sarah with the predatory intensity of someone who believed his mark was chosen long ago.

"What did Sarah uncover, Danny? What was she investigating?" James's voice was a furtive, controlled command as the storm's din wrapped around his words like a deadly secret.

Breath coming in rapid, fearful bursts, the boy answered with jittery urgency. "Records. Money laundering, illegal deals. And… kids disappearing from the estate like they're swallowed by the dark." The confession stumbled out as his terror escalated. "She said it reached the top—politicians, cops, everyone's in bed with them. She even had proof… but you can't fight that. They own all of it. Control everything."

As thunder unleashed its fury above, Danny shrank further into himself, his fragile frame curled tight like a wounded animal. "I'm sorry," he whispered amid a mingling of tears and rain. "I told her things I shouldn't have about the estate. About those empty flats… now… now she's dead because I couldn't keep quiet."

"No," James thundered in response, his voice a low growl that seemed to challenge the very rain. Clutching the boy's trembling shoulder, his own resolve hardened. "Sarah died because she dared to fight for what was right. The true monsters are the bastards who ended her life."

Reaching into his pocket, James extracted a card and pressed it into Danny's clammy hand. "Call me. If you see those men again or if anything feels wrong, day or night—I'll be there."

Danny's gaze lingered on the card as if it were the only lifeline in a sea of malevolence. "Why? Why are you doing this for me?" he asked, voice barely audible over the relentless downpour that now felt like the very claws of an accusation.

"Because Sarah believed in you," James replied, his tone brimming with a fierce, almost feral intensity. "I believe in her."

The boy managed a nod as desperation etched deeper lines into his face, tucking the card away like a relic of fragile hope. As James turned to depart, the rain—each drop now a brutal reminder of complicity—spattered his neck, cold like confession. Danny's voice, laden with dread, trailed after him: "They'll kill you too, just like they killed her."

Staring into the storm's wrath and into the abyss of that warning, James could only silently accept the truth. Death had long ceased to instill fear in a man who'd already tasted its bitter promise. Some truths, he knew, demanded a sacrifice.

With a resigned grimace, James started the engine. The Verve's haunting lyrics seeped into the dim interior, its melancholic refrain threading with the relentless pounding of malignant rain. The air around smelled faintly of Sarah's perfume—a light, floral scent that now mingled with decay and grief, or perhaps it was nothing more than a ghost conjured by memory.

In that moment, James felt a suffocating unity between his target and the corrupted world around him. Names and faces blurred into a vast tapestry—the scarred predator staring from the dark corners of rundown pubs, the black cars encircling council estates like vultures, and the omnipresent watchers whose gazes were as invasive as the dying light over Wokingham. He would pull at that thread until the whole grotesque tapestry unraveled, hallmarked by betrayal and decay—even if it meant the collapse of his own existence.

The Escort's headlights forged punch-bags of light in a rain of accusation, leaving behind a diminishing outline of Danny—a pitiful wanderer lost in Wokingham's intricate web of corruption and collusion. But James was far from retreating. Not while the dark heart of the city pulsed with secrets he was destined to unearth.

The tempest roared on, yet beneath its fury lay a perverse calm—a chilling clarity affirming that purpose had found him. Sarah had laid down her life to expose the clandestine poison festering at Wokingham's core. Now, it was his turn to follow her breadcrumbs into the abyss, to the ruins of Bellamy's Storage where decay and neglect reigned.

Parking in a deserted lot behind The Ship Inn, where warm light now mocked him from behind grimy windows, James's breath fogged the car's interior as he clutched Sarah's final journal entry. Retrieved from his flat in a haze of determined grief, its words burned with an urgency that matched the storm outside. There, penned in a hurried scrawl and dated three days before her death, were hints of dread: "Saw him again. The one with the scar. He was watching the estate from a black Mercedes. With someone, this time—someone official. Suit, better than my whole year's pay. The way they watched the kids... it made my skin crawl. Need to cross-check the council records again. M says there's a pattern... if you know where to look."

James's grip tightened on the timeworn notebook. M. It had to be Michael Reynolds, Sarah's liaison from the council—one who vanished on "extended leave" immediately after her death. Another thread in the noose of corruption.

A creak at the pub's back door announced Dave—a hulking figure wrapped in grim responsibility. "You better come in," he muttered, stepping into the cold, amber light that bled over the wet tarmac, his voice heavy with the weight of forbidden knowledge.

Inside, the back office of the pub resembled a forgotten confessional, its dark wood walls swallowing the scant light of an ancient desk lamp as if guarding their own sordid secrets. Dave locked the door, then hauled from beneath the desk a bottle of Macallan 18—the kind of luxury reserved for dire revelations.

"This was dropped off today," Dave said, pouring two generous measures. Sliding a manila envelope across the scarred desk, he added, "Guy who brought it, wasn't from around here, but he knew things. About Sarah. About what she was digging into."

James's hand, still trembling from the earlier encounter with Danny, reached for the envelope. Inside were photographs: grainy, black-and-white snapshots of Sarah caught in moments of desperate surveillance—outside The Holt School, at the market, entering her own flat. But the final image stamped a new terror onto his soul: Sarah at The Ship Inn on the fateful night, locked in a clandestine conversation with a shadow just beyond the frame.

"Look at the timestamps," Dave urged in a gravelly tone.

Every photo was annotated with precise dates and times—a meticulous chronicle of Sarah's final days. Yet, it was the accompanying handwritten note that knifed through the silence: "She didn't suffer. Remember that when choosing your next steps, Detective. Some questions are best left unasked."

"Bastards," James spat, the word echoing with decades of pent-up fury. "They're trying to scare me off."

Dave's face contorted with age and hardship. "There's more. That guy from last week—the one with the scar? He came by again today, asking about you."

"What did he ask?"

"Not questions—more like cautious threats cloaked in civility. He wanted to know about your routines, who you keep close, whether you're 'stable'." Dave's voice fell to a conspiratorial murmur. "They're shadowing you, building a case in case something happens."

James peered into the amber depths of his untouched whiskey. "They're afraid," he murmured. "Danny must know something critical. Something they can't risk speaking out."

"Or maybe they simply can't risk you piecing together what Sarah exposed," Dave added, his tone dropping to a mournful whisper. "Think about it—why take out a teacher? Unless she unearthed something more monstrous than missing children and dodgy money... something worth a killing."

"The council records," James affirmed as clarity struck him like a brutal truth. "Sarah mentioned a pattern, something in the planning department. Now Reynolds is on leave, records are sealed, and expensive cars stalk council estates under the cover of night."

"Development contracts," Dave offered, his voice brittle with disquiet. "Rumors of compulsory purchase orders, estates being earmarked for 'regeneration' that push out entire communities."

"Forcing people out, hiding the truth," James concluded, thoughts racing with grim coherence. "But what truth?"

Before Dave could speak, the office phone shattered the heavy silence with three sharp, menacing rings. Dave answered with his usual brusque greeting, then froze—the color draining from his face. After a pregnant pause, he pressed the receiver into James's grasp.

"Detective Thornton," purred a cultured voice, oozing confidence and fine breeding. "I believe it is time we had a civilized talk about boundaries. About letting sleeping dogs lie."

With clinical precision, James replaced the phone. The oppressive shadows of the office seemed now to pulse with covert menace, the dim light deepening into near abyss. Dave's features had taken on a corpse-like pallor under the feeble glow, his eyes hollows hinting at nothing less than infinite malice.

"They've woven themselves into every layer," James murmured, his voice strangely echoing in the quiet. "The force, the council, the schools...I can see it now. Sarah seen the entire rotting framework."

He clutched Sarah's journal—a beacon in the darkness—as its pages rustled like whispered confessions against his fingertips. The photographs spread before him were no mere images; they were tarot cards heralding doom and unraveling a tapestry of corruption and calculated predation. Every stolen moment of Sarah's final weeks now resonated as a scream in silence.

"There's one more thing," Dave said, rummaging beneath his desk. The metallic sound of a drawer sliding open was like the crack of a spinal column under strain. Emerging from the shadows was a battered mobile phone—Sarah's old Nokia 3210, its screen fractured like a spiderweb of regret. With a hesitant press, it sputtered to life, displaying its final log: a series of calls—a desperate reach to a school, to her sister, and, most damningly, to an unfamiliar number mere hours before her death. But it was the final text message that splintered James's resolve into shards of icy dread:

"Storage unit 23, Bellamy's. Midnight. Bring the files. Last chance to do this quietly."

"Bellamy's," James breathed with a shiver, his voice carrying the weight of unholy recognition, "the abandoned storage facility on Reading Road, owned by—"

"Marcus Renwick," Dave finished, his tone nihilistic. "A property developer with council ties, always a step ahead. The man who seems to know which estates are destined for 'regeneration' long before the official word."

Every piece now slotted into a harrowing tableau: development contracts, vanished children, black cars prowling like vultures—each element a thread in the vast, poisonous conspiracy that had seeped into every cracked crevice of Wokingham. The revelation struck James with the force of an oncoming freight train, his thoughts spiraling over the night's grim exchanges.

"She went there that night," James repeated, voice trembling with the horror of understanding. "She didn't go to the school like they said. She went straight to Bellamy's with the evidence—evidence that could unravel it all."

"And they waited for her," Dave's voice was a hollow echo of disbelief and horror. "They twisted her bravery against her. Her very commitment to justice became the weapon they used."

A cold sweat broke along James's brow as he abruptly rose, the chair's protest a screech against the worn floorboards. In that claustrophobic back office, heavy with the weight of unspeakable truths, every object and shadow seemed complicit, tightening around him like a noose of inevitability. The call, the photographs, Danny's terror—all converged to force this moment of grim clarity.

"I must go to Bellamy's," he declared through gritted teeth, already pressing toward the door. "Whatever Sarah uncovered, whatever she died for—it's all still there. It must be."

"James," Dave cautioned, his voice laden with foreboding. "They're watching. Waiting."

"I know," James said, his eyes hardening as he turned—a defiant glint ignited by his indomitable resolve. "Let them watch. Let them come. Some questions refuse to fade. Some deaths demand remembrance."

Stepping back into the malicious rain, each droplet now striking his face with the sting of accusation, James found solace only in his relentless pursuit of truth. The Escort waited like a dreaded hound in the gloom, its metal carcass reflecting sodium lights that contorted into leering, accusatory eyes.

Inside the car, the radio crackled unexpectedly, unleashing The Verve's spectral melody. Richard Ashcroft's voice reverberated like a doomed prophecy:

"Now the drugs don't work, they just make you worse..."

The engine growled in approval as James drove off into the tempest—a storm that was no mere weather pattern but a dark, sentient tribunal of guilt and retribution. Ahead lay Bellamy's Storage, a forsaken relic of industrial decay, where rusted corrugated metal and peeling signage bore silent witness to decades of abandonment and neglect. It was there, amid the oppressive stench of disuse and hidden secrets, that unit 23 waited with revelations as dark as the secrets festering within Wokingham itself—a city entrenched in a conspiracy as relentless and damning as the rain.

Every nerve on high alert, James parked in the desolate lot behind the facility—a crumbling, skeletal structure that whispered of bygone glory turned malignant ruin. The building's broken windows and faded labels were like the open wounds of a city in decay, its every creak and gust of wind a reminder of its sinister complicity in the crimes it sheltered.

With trembling determination, he unlocked unit 23 and swung wide the heavy, corroded door. Inside, amidst the detritus of a forgotten era, lay file after file brimming with incriminating evidence. And amidst the chaos of documents and filtrations of dust, one photograph shattered his remaining resolve: Sarah, lifeless on cold, indifferent concrete.

Tears blurred his vision as he acknowledged the terrible cost of her unyielding mission. Yet, as he turned to leave, the oppressive darkness coalesced into a shape—a shadowy figure emerging from the gloom, blocking his escape.

"Hello, James," the voice drawled, steeped in menace. "Did you really think you could outsmart us?"

In that frozen heartbeat, hope ebbed from James as the predator's gaze—psychologically invasive and predatory—seared into his soul. But defiance surged back. Clenching his fists in a silent vow, he squared his shoulders against the crushing weight of their power, resolved to fight, even if it cost him everything.

Some sacrifices, he realized, were inevitable—and necessary. Even if standing in defiance of an omnipresent, complicit system meant joining Sarah in the endless night.

And as the malevolent rain hammered relentlessly, each drop a brutal whisper of accusation, James stepped forward into the darkness, where answers and annihilation awaited in equal measure.

CHAPTER 6:
'THE RIVERBOAT
SONG' (PRESENT DAY)

The wooden sign of The Ship Inn groaned in the wind as James neared, its worn paint peeling away like layers of forgotten promises. He paused at the entrance, feeling an ache of familiarity amid the rapid pulse of modernity brushing past him. The din of uneasy laughter and low murmurings from inside mixed with the scent of damp, aging wood and sour, stale ale, setting an ominous undertone that clung to the pub like a shroud.

Stepping inside, James's eyes roamed the dim, smoke-hazed room until they fell upon Dave behind the counter—a man whose eyes bore a weight of regret as much as warmth. Time had etched its story into his features, and beneath his welcoming smile lay a hidden anguish. "James Thornton," Dave greeted, his voice trembling slightly as he set down a pint. "It's been too long." But even as he spoke, fragments of hushed conversations drifted through the air—snatches of whispers about debts unpaid, crimes unspoken, and a name that seemed to pierce the murk of the establishment.

James grasped Dave's hand firmly, noting the calluses that spoke of long years of relentless labor and unspoken guilt. "Sorry I haven't been back sooner," he replied, a rueful grin failing to mask the tremor in his voice.

Dave leaned in, his eyes flickering with an internal torment. "I know you didn't come here just for a drink and a catch-up," he observed quietly, as if weighing each word against the burden he carried—the guilt stemming from a night he wished he could forget, a moment when perhaps he might have done more for Sarah.

James sighed, the sound heavy within him, and slid onto a scuffed leather barstool. "No, I need your help with something," he confessed, his throat tightening.

At the mention of her name, the very air seemed to thicken. Dave's face contorted with a mixture of sorrow and remorse. "This is about Sarah, isn't it?" he whispered, his eyes darting nervously toward shadowed corners where dubious figures huddled and murmured unintelligible phrases—snatches like "organized..." and "shipment deadlines..." that hinted at something far more sinister than a simple tragedy.

James reached into his jacket, pulling out a crumpled scrap of paper and carefully smoothing it out on the bar. The crude eye symbol, scratched and blatant, gazed back like a mocking sentinel. "I've been spotting this everywhere," he explained, his voice edged with a rising urgency. "On flyers, doorframes... even, Danny— Sarah's student—mentioned that the men tracking her had it tattooed on their necks."

He looked at Dave with desperation etched into every line of his face. "Have you ever seen this symbol before? Do you know what it means?"

Dave's eyes narrowed as he studied the mark, and a shadow

darkened under his gaze. "Now that you mention it, I have seen it before," he admitted slowly. "About a month before... well, you remember." His voice faltered, burdened by the secret memory of that fateful encounter and the recognition of his own failure.

James leaned forward, his pulse pounding in his ears like a warning drumbeat. "Where? On who?" he pressed, the heat of anger and grief flaring in his veins.

Dave's whisper was almost lost in the clamor of muffled conversations. "A couple of guys... they'd come in often, seated all alone in that far corner booth. One—he bore the same tattoo right under his ear." Dave's hand unconsciously touched that spot on his face, as if to remind himself of the past he couldn't escape. "I assumed it was gang insignia, but now..." His voice trailed off as fragments of raucous chatter spilled from nearby patrons— snippets discussing "arrangements" and "big money" that made the air even heavier.

"Did you hear them talking?" James interjected, desperation tightening his throat. "Anything about Sarah or the academy?"

Dave shook his head, his eyes warily scanning the room as if expecting hidden spies among the murmuring crowd. "No. They said nothing outright," he replied, his tone laced with regret and a guilt that transcended mere memory.

A bitter disappointment sharpened James's words as he whispered, "Do you remember anything else at all?"

Dave furrowed his brow, his mind seemingly tormented by what he couldn't forget. "No... I'm sorry, that's all I have." His voice was heavy with remorse, as if each word was a nail in the coffin of his own inaction regarding Sarah's fate.

Grateful yet troubled, James nodded and tucked the scrap of paper back into his pocket. As he stepped out, the sinister presence of the symbol on the parchment gnawed at his resolve, urging him onward into the labyrinth of clues—a clue that now connected Sarah's death to something far more organized.

Dave's confession came in a hushed tremor, barely audible over the unsettling din of the pub. His gaze shifted incessantly, anxiety and dread mingling. "It wasn't random. It was organized crime," he murmured, voice shaking as he clutched his beer tighter. "They were negotiating with a wealthy businessman. I caught fragments —money talks, shipments... I couldn't hear it all, but everything reeked of danger."

A chill shot through James's veins as the pieces clicked in a brutal mosaic. Sarah's death had been no isolated tragedy; it was the fallout of a dangerous game, one in which she had unwittingly stepped in. "What was she involved in?" James thought, a storm of anger and grief surging through him. He swallowed the tumult of emotions—each beat of his heart echoing in his flesh, leaving his skin tingling with both cold fear and burning fury.

Suppressing the raw, visceral pain that crept up his throat like icy smoke, James forced the questions down, unwilling to risk tipping Dave further into panic. Yet, as he slid the paper away, a spark of determination emerged from the depths of his torment. Sarah's death could not be mired in silence; justice had to be exacted, and the organization behind it must be dismantled.

Rising from his seat with tremulous strength, James grasped Dave's shoulder in a gesture that was part gratitude, part shared burden. "I'll handle this," he declared, locking eyes with the man whose guilt-laden silence spoke volumes. "I know Sarah would demand nothing less."

Dave's eyes glistened with a mix of sorrow and self-condemnation. "She was a wonderful teacher, and a good soul," he whispered, barely audible amid furtive murmurs and sinister laughter from a nearby table where a hushed conversation hinted, "...money laundering, ... shipments from abroad..." that sent another shiver down James's spine. "What happened to her isn't right."

After one last, lingering squeeze of Dave's shoulder—an unspoken apology for his own failures—James stepped out into the cold, unforgiving night. The mist swallowed the neon glow as a familiar, heartbreaking melody drifted on the wind. The nostalgic strains of Ocean Colour Scene's "The Riverboat Song" filled the air, each note a dagger twisting in his heart. Memories of raucous car rides and joyful sing-alongs now clashed bitterly with the stark emptiness of loss.

Tears, unbidden and raw, slid down his cheeks as every heartbeat pounded with the weight of his grief. Amid the torrent of emotions, a terrible, searing anger ignited—a fury fueled by the memory of Sarah's relentless determination to change the world, even if it had cost her everything.

But then, his thoughts drifted to those still in peril—Danny isolated on his park bench, Miss Jenkins shattered by the loss of her daughter, and even Dave, who risked confronting dangerous shadows to seek the truth. They all depended on him now. Every step he took filled with the icy determination of a man who would not allow another innocent soul to be sacrificed.

Yet as James turned a corner into the darker alleys of the city, a foreboding truth loomed like a specter. In the reflective puddles at his feet, a message scrawled in red marker on a weathered wall unnervingly echoed the symbol on his paper: "Justice is a debt paid in blood."

That revelation was not just a warning—it was a promise of further violence, a clear and present threat that the forces behind Sarah's murder were watching, waiting to strike again. With his heart pounding and his body burning with equal parts despair and resolve, James stepped deeper into the mist, determined to unearth the conspiracy and avenge Sarah's death once and for all.

CHAPTER 7: 'THE BARTENDER & THE THIEF' (1999)

The Wokingham town hall had become a gilded prison that evening—a dazzling façade of light and sound concealing an atmosphere of quiet menace. Crystal chandeliers hung like frozen sentinels from a high, ornately carved ceiling, their golden glow casting long, oppressive shadows across the polished parquet floor. Amid the air of forced laughter and murmured conversation, every clink of glass seemed to echo like a punishment, a reminder of the underlying decay of wealth and deceit.

James could not shake the feeling of being hunted in this glittering trap. Clad in a rented tuxedo that felt nothing like his own worn jeans and faded t-shirt, he shifted uneasily, tugging at the tight collar as if it could free him from its suffocating grip. The bow tie constricted his throat like an accusation, the starched shirt a metaphorical straitjacket that hindered his every move. Surrounded by the town's elite—politicians and business magnates—he felt every eye on him, as if the room itself were part of an elaborate surveillance state, recording his every misstep.

Determined to unearth the twisted truths behind Sarah's murder, James navigated the glittering facades that masked decades of greed and exploitation. This was the world that had silenced

Sarah when she dared to expose the rot festering at its core —a world where the expensive veneer belied an underbelly of corruption and hidden agendas. With every overheard snippet of conversation, James felt the weight of unseen watchers pressing in. Murmurs about a lucrative new development at Finchampstead and whispered conspiracies about political favors echoed like threats meant only for him. Even amid the jovial clamor, an uncomfortable awareness settled over him: every smile, every glance, was a potential trap.

It was then that his gaze landed on a man in the far corner— a sharply dressed figure marked by a cruel scar slicing down his left cheek and a hint of an inked eye barely visible beneath his collar. There was a coiled strength about him that spoke of danger and unspoken orders. As James's heart pounded, the chilling realization gripped him: this was the man repeatedly whispered about by the unseen overlords, the one who had argued with Sarah on the night before her untimely death. The resurfacing memories of Sarah's defiance, her relentless quest for justice, merged with the oppressive ambiance of the gala into a single, searing indictment of a corrupt society.

Amid the sea of glittering deceptions, a hand grasped James's arm, yanking him aside. Miss Jenkins—whose normally placid composure was now clouded with something far more desperate and personal—pulled him into a shadowed alcove. Her eyes, usually steady and inscrutable, shimmered with a mix of anxiety and a secret burden that went beyond mere professional duty. For Miss Jenkins, this was not simply about aiding a determined man in his quest for justice; it was also an effort to atone for failures of her own—a deep, personal regret intertwined with her sense of duty, a desire to right the wrongs she had long been complicit in.

"Not here," she whispered urgently, her voice trembling under the oppressive weight of the secrets they both harbored. As they slipped away from the prying acoustics of the main hall, her trembling hands produced a crumpled receipt. It wasn't merely a slip of paper—it was a tangible shard of reality, a remnant of Sarah's final days. The paper, marked with a date three weeks before Sarah's death and emblazoned with the name of Bellamy's Storage, pulsed in James's hand like a dark heartbeat. In that moment, the ordinary receipt transformed into a symbol of betrayal and hidden terror, its significance exploding into clarity: Marcus Renwick, the slick property mogul whose wealth had shielded him from consequences, owned Bellamy's. Sarah's probing questions, once muffled by polite society, now rang out as clear indictments against a man who thrived on imperviousness and control.

The oppressive glamour of the gala, the murmuring conspiracies, and the understanding that he was being meticulously observed —all of it converged to connect the glittering event with Sarah's silenced dissent. Every whispered comment about the "Cooke girl" and every sly exchange concerning political favors now bore the unmistakable stench of complicity in her murder. Rage and grief roiled within James as the pieces of the puzzle snapped together— a mosaic of corruption, cruelty, and calculated power.

Despite the seething anger that urged him to confront the dangerous man immediately, James took slow, measured steps back into the throng. The murmurs around him seemed now like disjointed puzzle pieces, their meaning growing ever darker. He sensed the weight of unseen eyes, the surveillance of those who wished to remain hidden, pressing in from the shadows cast by glimmering chandeliers. Each forced smile and perfunctory greeting belied a world in which every move was recorded, every motive dissected.

Sarah's memory burned in his heart: a memory of defiance, of a soul who had fought for justice, even against overwhelming odds. As James rejoined the crowd, his gaze hardened with determination and dread, knowing that this lead—the crumpled, damning receipt held tightly in his hand—might be the key to exposing a far-reaching conspiracy. With a heavy resolve, he steeled himself against the psychological torture of his environment, ready to peel back the layers of corruption even as the room's glamorous oppression bore down upon him.

In the midst of the jubilant music that now felt like a cruel parody of celebration, James prayed he had enough strength to tear down the façade and confront those who had stolen Sarah's voice. The oppressive eyes of the gala—and perhaps something far more sinister—watched him, and he vowed not to falter. The time had come to confront the orchestrators of this malignant empire, and to force their treacherous secrets into the light.

CHAPTER 8: 'SHIVER' (PRESENT DAY)

The oppressive fog draped over Wokingham like a shroud, swallowing sounds and distorting every familiar landmark. James clutched his coat close, each step toward St. Crispin's School feeling as if it carried him deeper into a waking nightmare, the cold pricking his nerves with every breath. The gloomy morning, drained of color and hope, pulsed with a forbidding energy that churned uneasily in his gut.

Despite the heaviness of his memories, he fought to dismiss the rising panic. Doubt was a luxury he couldn't afford, not when the truth lay so perilously close.

Then the school materialized through the murk—a fortress of red brick and Gothic embellishments that seemed to leer at him with conspiratorial intent. The structure, with its sharp arches and gnarled spires, looked less like an institution and more like a cryptic guardian of ancient sins. Windows, dark and penetrating, bore down upon him with a silent accusation. A violent flutter of distress gripped James as he recollected the sorrow and torment intertwined with those walls—memories of grief, seething anger, and a guilt that clung to his bones. Sarah had once navigated these cold corridors, inhaling the same frigid air that now stifled him, and it was here that she had stumbled upon secrets that sealed her tragic fate.

With determination carved into every step, James ascended the stone steps and pushed open the heavy oak door, the creak of its hinges seeming almost like a lament. Inside, the hallways were steeped in unsettling silence; the usual vibrancy of student chatter replaced by the hollow echo of his footsteps on the polished floor, as if the building itself was mourning lost truths. Each step invoked flashes of memories—painful and vivid—that made his skin crawl and throat tighten.

Following a path etched into his muscle memory, he reached the headteacher's office. There, Mr. Thompson waited—a gaunt, tall man whose matted grey hair and weary eyes hinted at battles fought in secret corridors of the past. As James stepped in, Thompson rose slowly from behind his desk, offering a handshake that carried more resignation than courtesy. His voice, low and laden with unspoken regrets, broke the stillness.

"DI Thornton," Thompson said, his tone dry yet edged with something unacknowledged. "What brings you here?"

James sank into the creaky leather chair, feeling every shudder of his body's memory as he spoke. "I'm investigating Sarah Cooke's death. I need answers."

Thompson's eyebrow arched in discomfort, as though the case itself was a specter he'd rather forget. "It's been over twenty years," he murmured, his choice of words guarded, laden with unsaid implications. "I believed that case was long closed."

"Not for me," James replied, his voice thick with raw frustration. "I won't rest until I know the truth." His gaze hardened, a storm of memories colliding with the present.

For a moment, Thompson's eyes—framed by worn wire-rimmed glasses—flickered with something almost like guilt or fear. In that brief glance, it was clear he knew more than he dared to reveal. Finally, with a reluctant nod that seemed to carry a monumental weight, he said, "How can I aid you?"

Leaning forward, elbows resting on his knees as if bracing against a tidal wave of memories, James pressed, "Did Sarah ever mention anything unusual? Anything at all—concerns or incidents that might have seemed out of place?"

Thompson's brow knit in troubled recollection. "She did come to see me about a week before her death. There was something in her eyes—an unsettled, jagged anxiety." His words lingered, heavy with unsaid details. "She requested time off, citing personal matters, but I got the distinct impression she was frightened... perhaps of someone or something lurking just beyond her sight."

The words struck James like a physical blow. His heart hammered as he inquired, "Did she mention any names, any concrete details?"

Thompson shook his head slowly, as if the memory itself pained him. "No, nothing explicit. But a few days later, a man appeared at the school, claiming to be a prospective guardian. He asked incessant questions about Sarah—her routines, her whereabouts." His voice dropped, the room seeming to tighten with the weight of his confession. "He was tall, with dark, unruly hair and a menacing presence. A scar cut sharply down his cheek, its edges still vividly red, as though it had been inflicted recently—a mark that made him seem predatory, like a beast lurking in the dark." In a gesture that betrayed a sorrow deeper than mere concern,

Thompson ran his fingers along his own cheek, mirroring the phantom scar. "I never trusted him. When I dared broach the subject, Sarah dismissed it. Told me to drop it, as if that about-face could erase the dread."

Every word sent tremors through James. His fists clenched until flesh met bone, the recognition of that scarred man igniting a raw, burning fury inside him. He'd seen that predator before—the same man from The Ship, the relentless watcher whose presence had tormented Sarah. The shards of his memory slotted together into a grim tableau, each piece reinforcing the sinister picture that began to take shape.

"Thank you," James managed, voice tight with contained rage, as he stood, careful not to expose the tumult beneath his composed exterior. "You've been…helpful."

Rising, Thompson's eyes softened briefly into an expression of conflicted remorse. "DI Thornton… James. I wish you well, but be cautious. Sarah wandered into dangerous territory—places and dark people best left unexplored. I fear if you stray too close, you might pay the same price." His warning was an echo of his own buried regrets, carrying an unspoken admission of his complicity.

Meeting those eyes with steely determination, James declared, "I have to do this. For her."

Thompson's shoulders slumped, heavy with both concern and a secret that gnawed at him. "I know… just—watch your back."

James left the office with a mind cluttered by haunting secrets and renewed purpose. Outside, the mist had thickened, swirling around his feet like spectral fingers, while unseen eyes glued themselves to his every step. The atmosphere shifted from mere physical threat to a relentless psychological siege.

Lost in his racing thoughts, he almost missed the vibration in his pocket. Pulling out his mobile, he glanced at the screen with a sinking heart. A new message from an unknown number flashed in a sinister green: "Step away before the shadows claim you completely—follow her end to find your own."

The words slithered under his skin, dredging up every ounce of raw terror and guilt he had fought so long to bury. They were not just a threat; they were a manipulation designed to seep into his soul, to make him doubt every step he took. James's pulse thundered in his ears as the realization struck—someone was hunting not only his body but his very psyche.

With a fierce grip that turned his knuckles to white, he shoved the phone back into his pocket. The threat only sharpened his resolve; he was far from being a rookie, vulnerable to empty menaces. Twenty-five years of relentless pursuit, scarred by every injustice, left him unyielding in his pursuit of justice for Sarah. No threat, no curse, would brake his determination.

Slamming the office door behind him, James reemerged into a world cloaked in swirling mist and ominous silence. The fog had grown denser, writhing like ancient spirits around his feet as he made for his car. Each step along the deserted street filled him with the relentless sensation of unseen eyes tracking his every move—not merely in space, but deep within the recesses of his mind.

He scanned the grey horizon, every nerve alert to potential danger, until he reached his worn Ford Escort. The engine roared to life amid the melancholy strains of Coldplay's "Shiver"—the song's plaintive chords echoing the unresolved grief and burning vengeance fueling him. "So I look in your direction, but you pay me no attention..." the lyrics murmured in his head, a grim reminder of his solitary path.

Behind the wheel, his grip was as tight as his resolve, every memory of missed chances and lost protections for Sarah pressing down upon him. In the billowing fog, a surreal clarity descended; the dark truth of what had beenfall her, the monstrous corruption, and the unseen forces now stalking his every waking moment.

The Escort accelerated, slicing through the mist with determined ferocity. The world blurred past as James' thoughts fixated on the leads ahead: the cavernous storage facility, the enigmatic scarred man, and the intricate web of secrets that had doomed Sarah. Flares of memory—of Danny, isolated and broken on a rain-drenched bench; of Miss Jenkins, eyes forever haunted by sorrow; of Dave, risking everything in a futile tribute—spurred him forward.

They were counting on him. And he would not betray their trust. The ominous buzzing of his phone punctuated the journey—a fresh message now glared back at him, dexterously designed to invade his thoughts further. James's lips curled in a bitter scoff as his resolve steeled even more firmly. If intimidation was their weapon, he would counter with unyielding ferocity.

The Escort roared onward, "Shiver" fading into the background, replaced by the relentless drumming of his engine. Every mile felt like a step deeper into the labyrinth of hidden horrors, yet he pressed forward. Eyes fixed on the horizon, every fiber of his being vibrated with the promise of retribution, and the whispered threat of vengeance growing louder with every passing moment.

Come what may, he was ready. And those who sought to haunt his past and obstruct his future would soon learn the true cost of their dark secrets.

CHAPTER 9:
'CREEP' (1999)

The fluorescent lights at Wokingham Police Station no longer simply illuminated the corridors—they loomed overhead like a judgmental jury, casting a sickly pallor over the institutional green walls that seemed to close in with every step. James stood in the hallway, his reflection distorted and ghostlike against the reinforced glass of the incident room. The gaunt face staring back evoked a stranger more than a reflection—dark circles whispered of sleepless nights and a frayed spirit, his tie hanging loosely as if in submission, while his usually impeccable shirt was crumpled and disheveled from countless hours poring over case files.

This station, once a sanctuary of purpose and brotherhood, had morphed into a realm of psychological confinement. Every corner exuded a sense of dread; the hushed murmurs that echoed down the halls, the furtive glances laden with barely concealed scorn, and the deliberate avoidance by colleagues all painted a picture of systematic ostracism. Since Sarah's passing, the atmosphere had crystallized into something colder—a creeping frost that obscured clarity, much like frost etching patterns that made it impossible to see the truth behind the glass.

Outside the cramped kitchenette, where the stench of burnt toast and cheap coffee mingled with stale despair, James paused. Through the small opening, he heard two officers—PC Mike Collins and DS Alan Peters—whose tones had shifted from friendly banter over pints at The Ship Inn to conspiratorial whispers muted by the oppressive environment.

"It's getting ridiculous, isn't it?" Collins murmured, his voice low and edged with contempt.

"He just won't let it go," Peters replied, his thick Yorkshire drawl now filled with disapproval, "and DCI Watson, he thinks James is spiraling—seeing conspiracies in every shadow."

"I heard DI Grant told him to drop it," Collins added with a dismissive shrug. "Says it's bad for morale. Nobody wants someone digging around where they shouldn't."

"Can you blame him?" Peters countered, barely masking his unease. "After what happened to her... Still, he needs to get his head in order."

The conversation fell silent as James's elongated shadow cut across the doorway. He lingered there, feeling the weight of unspoken accusations before moving down the corridor that seemed to stretch infinitely, each echo of his footfall hammering home the feeling of being systematically buried by the very institution he had once trusted.

Inside the morning briefing room, the oppressive air thickened; the room was dim despite the forced brightness, filled with officers in blue who wore exhaustion like a second skin. Cigarette smoke clung stubbornly in spite of "No Smoking" signs plastered on the walls, a sign of shared dissent and simmering anxiety. Heads briefly lifted as James entered, only to drop again when they registered his presence—a subtle yet explicit act of avoidance.

At the head of the room, DI Peter Grant sat with a heaviness that belied his stubborn efficiency. His frame, clad in a rumpled suit from M&S that seemed a mute testament to wasted better days, betrayed nothing of the turbulence within. As he pored over a case file, a tightness in his shoulders deepened when he heard the door click open. His voice, when he finally spoke, carried an ambiguous blend of authority and regret as he addressed James.

"Thornton," he said coolly, not meeting his eyes. "What are you doing here? You're not scheduled for this briefing."

Ignoring the furtive whispers of colleagues who trailed behind him like specters, James stepped closer. "I need to speak with you—about Sarah Matthews. In private, sir."

A heavy silence engulfed the room. Grant's jaw tightened, one small muscle twitching in an expression that tried desperately to mask his inner conflict. Slowly, as if each word was a reluctant concession, he closed the file and turned fully to James.

"We've already discussed this," Grant stated in measured, clipped tones. "The Matthews case is closed—the evidence speaks for itself."

"What evidence?" James retorted, his tone steeling with anger. "A few tire marks, half-baked witness statements, and loosely tied assumptions? There's more, I know it."

Grant's eyes narrowed, and for a fleeting second, his gaze swept over the room—a silent plea for understanding from his peers, now turned silent judges—before locking back on James. "My office. Now."

Each step toward Grant's office felt like a march toward oblivion. The corridor, under the glare of oppressive lights and the weight of countless unsaid accusations, morphed into an endless tunnel. Inside, the diminutive space was cluttered with chaotic piles of case files and empty coffee cups, each item a relic of decades of unresolved secrets and institutional decay. As Grant clicked the door shut, the sound resonated like a death knell.

"Sit down, James," Grant ordered, his hand gesturing vaguely toward a battered chair. The simple command belied a deeper torment—a man caught between his duty and a personal history that too often blurred ethical lines.

James remained standing. "I have new information, sir. About the man with the scar arguing with Sarah outside The Ship. And the symbol—the eye. It's everywhere. It can't be coincidence."

"James..." Grant began, his tone softening momentarily, laden with a gravitas that suggested concern—perhaps a desire to protect him from a spiral he knew all too well. "I realize how much Sarah meant to you. We all cherished her. But this fixation, it's dangerous. You're seeing patterns where there are none, conjuring connections instead of facts."

"But are they?" James pressed, producing Sarah's battered notebook from within his jacket. Its pages, yellowed and dog-eared, bore the weight of her relentless pursuit of truth. "She was onto something massive, sir—so big that it cost her her life. The threats, the covert surveillance, her erratic behavior in those final weeks... they all scream of a conspiracy."

"Enough!" Grant slammed his fist on the desk, the staccato thud reverberating off the walls. The impact rattled not only the heavy metal nameplate declaring him Detective Inspector but also the fragile hope that integrity still held any sway. "I've been patient, James. Because of your connection to Sarah, because I know the caliber of detective you are. But this ends now."

Leaning forward, his face flushed with a volatile mix of frustration and something darker—a sorrow perhaps, or warning —Grant continued, "You can't always hunt for meaning in every tragedy. Sometimes, terrible things just happen. There isn't always a grand design, just random misfortune and the heavy burden of guilt."

Something inside James broke like brittle glass. "Is that what they told you? The same people who buried this investigation before it had a chance to breathe? The ones ensuring leads were stifled before they could even flicker?"

Grant flinched, his eyes betraying a moment of inner conflict, a hint of the man who once believed in absolute justice. But then his expression hardened, morphing back into the impenetrable mask of authority that now shielded his inner torment. "That's enough, Sergeant. You're treading on dangerous ground. Effective immediately, you're on administrative leave. Get your head straight—speak to the department counselor. If you continue down this path... there won't be a place for you here."

James looked at the man before him—the mentor who had once extolled the virtues of truth at any cost—and saw only a hollow bureaucrat, his passion quelled by a system more interested in preserving its image than uncovering the truth.

The burning trail of whiskey slowly purged the acrid residue of betrayal from James's mouth as he muttered, "Administrative leave," each word heavy with forced resignation and quiet rage. "So, they think I'm fabricating conspiracies out of thin air. I need to clear my head."

Across town in The Ship Inn, the atmosphere was far from innocent. When Dave noticed James's arrival, he set aside the bottle he was polishing glasses with, his rugged face etched with concern and the weariness of too many silent battles. "Blimey, mate," Dave exclaimed, reaching for another bottle as if it were a weapon, "you look like you've been chased by your own demons."

James, taking his usual place on a creaking barstool that groaned under the weight of his burdens, replied with a weary contemplation, "Perhaps I have... seen more than I ever thought this job was meant to be about."

Dave poured a generous measure of whiskey, his eyes darkening as he leaned in conspiratorially. "They're not just trying to keep you away, James. There's something dirty festering in Wokingham —corruption that runs deeper than petty discipline. I've seen it myself: strange figures lurking in the night, whispers of cover-ups, and officers who scatter like frightened animals at the mere mention of your name."

The dim, foggy light filtering through the pub's ancient windows lent the moment a spectral quality, as if the old building harbored the secrets of every misdeed ever committed within the precincts of power. James's voice dropped to a grim murmur. "Do you really believe there's more to it? That Sarah's death wasn't just another tragic accident?"

Dave's eyes glinted with a mix of hardened resolve and sorrow, his voice low and urgent. "Absolutely. It's all connected—the silencing of dissent, the deliberate smothering of leads, and the way this town has been bought and sold right under our noses. They've engineered this isolation, James. You're not just a rejected officer; you're a threat, a loose end they need to tie up."

As the melancholic strains of Radiohead's "Creep" crackled from an ancient jukebox, James raised an amber-hued glass in silent defiance. His gaze held a steely promise. "I won't relent. I'll find out the truth, no matter how deep the rot goes."

Dave clinked his glass against James's, the sound echoing in the silenced corners of the pub—a pact forged in mutual disillusionment. "Then count me in, whatever you need, mate. We're in this together."

In that charged silence, as the oppressive weight of Wokingham's corruption and systemic isolation threatened to crush him, James realized that every step forward was a battle against an institution that had once been his home. He left the pub with a resolve as unyielding as diamond, even as the neon glare of the police station, the hushed, hostile whispers of colleagues, and notes of insidious betrayal played on in his mind—a constant reminder that he was alone in fighting a darkness that had enshrouded everything he once believed in.

CHAPTER 10: 'NO SURPRISES' (PRESENT DAY)

The early morning light barely broke through the oppressive, heavy curtains that guarded James's flat—a space that no longer felt merely rundown, but violated, as if intruders had rummaged through its very soul. Every surface seemed tarnished by a residue of neglect and intrusion—the grimy walls bore the scars of past transgressions like invasive graffiti etched into their decay.

James sat, a shadow of his former self, hunched over the kitchen table. His hands gripped a mug of lukewarm coffee as if clutching at the remnants of a lost lifeline, yet the bitter taste only stirred a torrent of memories. There, spread before him like a desecrated altar, were shards of his past: Sarah's diary, its pages ruined by tears and time; faded police reports that documented a history he could neither deny nor escape; and the haunting photos of Sarah —her once brilliant eyes now void, as if a malevolent force had drained them of life.

The flat pulsed with an unnerving energy, each creak of the floorboards and whisper of stale air echoing like a threat. Overhead, shadows seemed to shift with deliberate intent, and James couldn't shake the overwhelming sensation that eyes— cold and calculated—were tracking his every move. He imagined hidden cameras or silently lurking figures observing his doubts and fears from the depths of the dark corners.

James's mind churned beneath the crushing weight of guilt and sorrow. Sleep had become a distant memory, replaced by relentless visions of Sarah's final days—her gaunt frame, her constant, terrified glances as if someone unseen pursued her at every turn. Now, he felt that same ever-watchful menace creeping closer with each heartbeat.

The oppressive silence was shattered by a soft, deliberate creak from outside his apartment door. Frozen, heart hammering in a staccato rhythm, James inched to the window. Below, in the murky streetlight, a figure in a dark coat and flat cap loitered —a presence unmistakably eerie. The figure's slow, scanning movements, the casual yet unnerving shift of weight as if listening for someone's approach, confirmed what James had long feared: he was being meticulously watched.

Panic erupted within him as he scanned his surroundings for any semblance of defense, his hand hovering above the drawer where his old service gun lay concealed. But before his trembling fingers could close the distance, a sharp knock reverberated at the door, shattering his fragile composure.

Spinning around, his eyes wild with terror and vulnerability, James braced himself for a host of ominous possibilities—a stranger with ill intent, a sinister figure from the pub, or one of the enigmatic shadows that had haunted him. Slowly and silently, he crept toward the door, each step weighted by dread. Through the peephole, relief washed over him upon recognizing Dave's familiar face. Yet, there was something in Dave's somber eyes, a glimmer of uncertainty that hinted at secrets unsaid.

"Jesus, what happened to you? You look like you've been visited by the devil himself," Dave said, his tone laced with concern—but also carrying an undercurrent that made James hesitate, a subtle reminder that trust might be a luxury they no longer possessed fully.

James forced a hollow laugh, though his grip on the moment remained frayed. "Close enough," he murmured, beckoning Dave inside. Keeping his voice low, he gestured toward the window. "Someone's been watching me."

Dave arched an eyebrow and moved to the window with measured steps. Peering out, his expression darkened as he questioned, "Did you see a man in a dark coat and flat cap?" His tone, though seemingly simple, carried the weight of unspoken past disappointments and a hidden agenda that James couldn't quite decipher.

"Yes, I saw him," James replied, uncertainty mingling with a growing dread.

"They were lurking outside the pub last night. And again the night before," Dave continued, shaking his head slowly, his disapproval mingled with a hint of something else—remorse, perhaps, or even unvoiced ambition. "I never trusted that look, and I doubt it's a mere coincidence with those harassing messages."

James ran a rough hand over his face, exhaustion mingling with burgeoning resolve. "I'd bet my sanity it's all part of a plan to break me—to push me until I give in."

Dave turned from the window, his eyes honing in with

an intensity that blurred the line between support and manipulation. "Well, if that's their aim, it's backfiring. Instead of breaking you, it's lighting a fire. But be cautious, James—I'm here, though you know trust isn't ever absolute."

A bitter, ironic smile touched James's lips, acknowledging Dave's ambiguous loyalty all too well. "I appreciate that, even if I sometimes wonder if you're with me or on the other side. But whoever's behind this is terrified. I'm on the verge of something big—a truth they'll do anything to bury."

Returning to his cluttered table, he sifted through scattered documents and mementos like a detective piecing together a conspiracy. "It all circles back to one symbol—the eye. Sarah's diary is a manifesto against it. And that threatener at the pub had a tattoo of it, unmistakable."

Dave leaned over, scrutinizing the cryptic notes, his frown deepening as he murmured, "And what about that storage unit —Bellamy's, right? Owned by that shadowy figure Renwick. It all tangles together: Renwick, the council, those developers prowling the old estates. Sarah stumbled onto something explosive, and they silenced her to keep their secrets safe."

James's knuckles whitened as his fist clenched in a mix of sorrow and raw determination. "She died for this, Dave. For doing what had to be done. I owe her justice."

Dave's hand rested on his shoulder, warm yet firm, though there was a subtle tension that spoke of unspoken dealings. "She was a beacon, a true soul among us. And you're carrying that light forward, aren't you? You're chasing her justice—even if sometimes it feels like you're driving us all into danger."

Their eyes met, and for a heartbeat, the shared past of brotherhood and betrayal lay bare between them. "I'm not sure I have it in me anymore, Dave. It's been so long; I'm not the man I once was."

Dave's grip tightened, a flash of both genuine care and a guarded intensity that hinted at hidden motives. "James Thornton, you are that man. The one who fought when the world conspired to crush you. Still, you must tread carefully—both the darkness outside and the one inside you."

A glance toward Sarah's faded photograph—her image both a memory and a silent charge—stirred James. "Do you think she'd want us to cower? To let these bastards win?"

Dave's eyes, gleaming and inscrutable, met his. "Not in a million years. She'd demand blood, if that's what it takes." His voice, though encouraging, carried an undertone that made James wonder if Dave's own demons would one day demand their due.

Just then, the shrill ring of James's phone sliced through the tension. James snatched it up to read the text, each word burrowing into his mind:

You think you can outrun your destiny, Thornton? Your secrets will drown you. Keep fighting, and watch your soul unravel.

The chilling message left his heart pounding and his resolve hardening. "They're trying to break me psychologically, Dave— invading every part of my mind. They won't win."

Dave's eyes, half reassuring and half calculating, locked onto his. "Damn right, mate. But remember, we're in this together—even if the truth of our alliance isn't as pure as we'd wish."

James inhaled deeply, the air of his violated flat mingling with his rising rage. Outside, the town awoke with indifferent clamor, unaware of the storm brewing within these walls. The once-silent corridors of deceit were about to resound with the noxious truth of betrayed lives and suppressed justice.

Enough was enough. The years of hiding, the invasive paranoia, were done. It was time to drag the darkness into the unforgiving light and cross the point of no return.

Steeling himself, James rose with an unyielding stance. His trembling hands of past fear transformed now into fists of resolve. "Let them watch," he declared, his voice a mix of fury and finality. "I'm done hiding."

Dave, his loyalty as ambiguous as the shadows in his own eyes, nodded slowly. "That's the James Thornton I recognize—the man beyond retreat."

A dry laugh escaped him—a morsel of humor amidst the chaos. "I'd better learn how to quit, though. Otherwise, who knows what I'll become..." He trailed off, barely concealing the weight of someone he once feared might claim his fate.

Dave's supportive yet enigmatic presence leaned in, his tone firm and layered with unspoken promises, "I won't let you fall. Or at least, I'll watch you rise, no matter the cost."

Their bond, as heavy and shifting as the secrets within the flat, fortified James for the coming battle. As if summoned by fate itself, his phone buzzed again with another spiteful message. With a cold fury igniting in his veins, he tossed it aside, the words burning into his mind.

"They think they can threaten my sanity, but they've never seen true defiance," he whispered, eyes locking on Dave's—both a mirror of mutual trust and a reminder that alliances can be as treacherous as the foes they fought.

Together, they stepped toward the door and into the relentless morning. With each determined stride, James felt himself crossing an irrevocable threshold—a point where retreat was no longer an option. He was no longer a man haunted by his past; he was a force driven by a need for retribution and truth.

The day had come. Today, James Thornton would confront every demon, every hidden watcher, every psychological torment. And as he marched forward, Dave—ever-present yet mystifyingly uncertain in his allegiance—shadowed him. With a final, resolute look, James stepped into the light, knowing that the storm he unleashed would spare no one in its catastrophic wake.

CHAPTER 11: 'DISCO 2000' (1999)

The Wokingham community centre, ordinarily a drab utilitarian space, had been shrouded in festive illusions for the annual charity gala—but beneath the glittering fairy lights and cheery decor, an undercurrent of foreboding pulsed through its very walls. Beneath the twinkling luminescence that bathed the room in an inviting glow, heavy shadows clung stubbornly to the corners, as though concealing whispered secrets. Round tables, dressed in immaculate white cloths and bedecked with pale roses and baby's breath, seemed to mask an unsettling void lurking behind their carefully arranged beauty. In one shadowed corner, a makeshift bar buzzed with quiet vigilance, its volunteers in black waistcoats and bow ties glancing around as if they too sensed that not everything was as it seemed.

On the small stage at the far end of the hall, a local band launched into an impassioned rendition of Pulp's "Disco 2000," their loud covers punctuated by cheers. But even amid the raucous energy of the performance, discreet cameras and pairs of unblinking eyes —hidden in the rafters and behind one-way panels—scrutinized every movement, as if the night itself was keeping score.

Amid this orchestrated revelry stood James Thornton, a solitary figure in a perfectly tailored rented tuxedo, clutching a flute of champagne. His outward composure belied a turmoil within, as his eyes roved the room with the predatory focus of a cornered animal. His isolation was a palpable chasm, deepening with every forced smile and each calculated glance. He wasn't merely mingling at a charity event; he was a man entrapped in his own relentless pursuit for truth. Caught within the ornate, pompous celebration, his purpose was singular—to uncover why Sarah's investigation had cost her everything.

His gaze fixed on a cluster of men near the stage. Their designer suits and self-important air set them apart, the very personification of the elite class. At their center stood Councillor Ward, whose impeccably slicked-back hair and condescending smirk were as emblematic of his persona as his rumored involvement in bypassing civic oversight. Flanking him was Richard Morton, a local property developer known not just for managing estates across counties, but for being a key conspirator in the backroom deals Sarah had meticulously documented. Every whispered word between them—hinting at redevelopment projects too conveniently timed and shady permits issued in secret—was a damning echo of the evidence Sarah had gathered.

Fury churned in James's chest as he tightened his grip on his champagne flute, his jaw set in grim determination. Sarah's notes had repeatedly implicated Morton in illicit schemes designed to exploit the vulnerable, her warnings now sounding like a death knell in every syllable. She had probed too deeply, and James was here on that same dangerous precipice.

A gentle, yet resolutely firm hand interrupted his spiraling thoughts as it rested on his arm. Helen Armitage stood beside him, her eyes reflecting more than concern—a steely mixture of regret and resolve mingled with the sorrow of shared grief. No longer just a gentle friend, Helen had become a clandestine ally in Sarah's fight—a former investigator in her own right, left with the burden of knowing too much.

"James," she murmured, her voice a blend of tenderness and a controlled urgency that spoke of sacrifices made in hushed confidences. "I didn't expect to see you here. This isn't your usual haunt, is it?"

There was a flicker in her eyes, a hardened glint that betrayed her intimate knowledge of the forces at work behind the gala's façade. They had spent countless nights, away from prying eyes, poring over Sarah's documents and connecting dots that many had hoped would remain buried. Her worry was not just for his safety—it was a silent accusation of responsibility, a reminder of the cost they'd already incurred.

James managed a small smirk—the closest he could muster to returning warmth—before replying hoarsely, "Not exactly. But I thought it might be a good opportunity to... talk to the right people. About Sarah."

As Helen's eyes swept cautiously toward the huddled group by the stage, a tremor of fear touched her voice. "James, I know you want answers. We all do. But those men... they're not only dangerous, they're calculated. They trample aside anyone who gets in their way. Every move here is observed."

Her words, heavy with forewarning born of her past in covert investigations, only deepened the isolation James felt. His solitude was not of his own choosing—it was a bitter tomb forged by betrayal and loss. "I can take care of myself," he snapped unexpectedly, then reached out, softening his tone as his hand squeezed hers in a silent plea for mutual support. "I know you're worried, Helen, but I can't let this go. I won't rest until I uncover why she died."

Helen's gaze held his for a long, somber moment, echoing back her own inner torment and unspoken secrets. "Just be careful," she urged, her grip tightening—not merely as a friend's concern but as a partner burdened by the weight of shared vengeance. "Sarah wouldn't want you to become another casualty in their game."

James's throat tightened with the lump of despair and determination. "I'll be careful," he whispered, feeling the words like embers in his mouth. "I must see this through. Understand?"

Her smile, filled with tragic resolve and dotted with tears that threatened to spill, answered silently. "Of course. If anyone can tear down their veneer, it's you. But remember, James, not all of us are fools. There are those who still care—people who need you to come home." With one final, solemn squeeze of his arm, she melted back into the throng, leaving him alone with the ghosts of regret and a mission that felt increasingly like a descent into a labyrinth of isolation.

Finishing his last sip of champagne, James set the empty glass onto a waiter's tray and straightened his posture as if bracing for an imminent battle. In this ornate nightmare, the power brokers were not mere street thugs but shadowy figures who controlled Wokingham's underbelly, ready to extinguish any light that threatened their dominion—even if it meant murder.

Quietly, he slinked through the crowd toward the contentious group near the stage. Overlapping conversations—furtive whispers about a new river development that would upend the town, veiled threats against a meddling journalist from the Chronicle, and hushed mentions of the "Cooke girl" who had ventured too close to their secrets—seeped into his ears. His heart pounded in response to those dangerous utterances, each fragmented sentence fanning the flame of his resolve, even as the band's next set drowned the clues in raucous noise.

Grinding his teeth, James forced himself to move further, acutely aware that every step could raise suspicion amid a sea of surveilling eyes. The gala's orchestrated merriment now seemed a meticulous performance, every guest both participant and watcher, every smile hiding apprehension.

His eyes fell on Dave Swinton—a familiar figure near the bar, always vigilant amid the layered deceptions. A momentary surge of relief bolstered his weary heart as Dave raised his glass in a conspiratorial gesture, eyebrow arched in silent inquiry. In that wordless exchange, Dave communicated that their silent pact would continue later, when safety allowed for discreet dialogues away from the invasive spotlight of this night.

With a heavy exhale, James slipped from Dave's line of sight and began pacing once more, his thoughts churning as he tried to piece together the convoluted network of evidence they had painstakingly gathered. There was no room for idle chatter here; every glance, every stray comment could mean imminent peril. The hunters were circling, masked by wealth and influence.

Instead, he edged toward the exit, senses alert to every furtive stare and covert surveillance subtlety—a cold reminder that the gala was less a celebration and more a theater of controlled chaos. Stepping into the cool night air, James drew in a lungful of the dark, crisp breeze, his eyes scanning the desolate streets of Wokingham that now betrayed nothing of their hidden corruption. The quaint town lay quiet, but beneath that placid exterior lurked a seething network of secrets.

At its core was Sarah—a radiant soul extinguished far too soon by the ruthless machinations of greed and power. Figures such as Ward and Morton, ensconced in their elegant suits and backroom dealings, treated lives like trivial pawns in their insidious games. Sarah had stared deep into that abyss and, in doing so, had awakened its callous wrath. Now it was James's burden to confront the darkness head-on, to pry open the hidden truths and lay bare the sins of those untouchable figures.

He knew the path ahead was treacherous—a tightrope walk through a web of surveillance, duplicity, and cold-blooded violence. Yet as he squared his shoulders and faced the biting wind, every step he took was a declaration of defiance. Behind him, the community centre glowed with a deceptive radiance—a carnival of lights and laughter contrived to mask the malevolence beneath.

James was done with pretense. He was determined to rip away the festive disguise and reveal the corruption festering within this world. For Sarah, for all that she had believed in, he would make those responsible pay—a solitude driven not by despair alone, but by the fierce conviction of a man left with no alternative.

CHAPTER 12: 'KARMA POLICE' (PRESENT DAY)

The Ship Inn no longer offered sanctuary but instead bore the taint of ceaseless investigation. What once felt like a haven was now a somber stage for secrets and whispered fears. As James pushed open the heavy oak door, he was immediately struck by an unsettling mix—the clink of glass punctuated by furtive glances and murmurs that carried a note of desperation. Far from the gentle, familiar hum of a refuge, the pub now reeked of spilled blood, stale beer, and an undercurrent of chemical cleaners desperately scrubbing away stains that no one dared mention.

The usual warmth of polished wood was replaced by the sterile scent of disinfectant and a stale odor of decaying evidence, as if the walls themselves were trying to erase the horrors they harbored. Each worn table bore fresh scratches that spelled out coded warnings—numbers and symbols hastily etched into the surface. Regulars clustered in small, wary groups, their pints trembling in hands that knew secrets far too grim for idle chatter.

James navigated through the dim light to his usual booth, though it now seemed more like a station at a crime scene than an escape from the cold world. His arrival did not go unnoticed; patrons exchanged anxious looks, their eyes darting not only at him but also toward shadowed corners where faces seemed to merge with the dark. In Wokingham, every whispered conversation carried the weight of eyes silently judging every move, as if the town itself were complicit, constantly surveilling every desperate act.

At the scarred booth, James slid into the vinyl seat with a heavy sigh, barely registering Dave Swinton's approach. Dave's steps were hesitant, his gaze flickering over the remnants of a hastily abandoned investigation—documents folded and hidden beneath the counter, a half-burnt cigarette lodged in the ashtray. When he set two pints on the scarred table, his sigh deepened, mingling with the ambient tension of a place that knew too much.

"You look like you've been dragged through hell," Dave remarked, his eyes scanning not only James's tired face but also the disturbing evidence scattered about—a smear of blood here, a stray photograph of a shattered window there. "When was the last time you got some decent sleep?"

James offered a hollow, bitter laugh, knowing full well that sleep had long ceased to be a companion. "Sleep's become a myth," he replied, the cool glass a feeble anchor in the torrent of his thoughts. His hand tightened around the pint. "I'll rest only when I see justice done. Only when I expose those responsible for Sarah's death."

Dave's face etched with a mix of sorrow and hardened resolve softened slightly. His memories of Sarah resonated in dings and murmurs within the creaking walls—a call to end the pervasive corruption that now seemed to seep from every surface. "I know you will," he said softly, leaning forward until his elbows rested on the stained tabletop. "But you have to play it smart. You're twirling dangerously close to the edge."

James's grip on his glass rattled his resolve, his knuckles blanching white. "I'm fully aware, Dave. I'm not naive enough to underestimate them." His words hung in the heavy air, underscored by the clamor of a town that seemed to conspire against him.

Dave's tone was a grudging whisper. "These aren't your run-of-the-mill crooks. We're talking about men who profit from misery —men who wouldn't hesitate to bury evidence beneath layers of cash and influence." A chill crept along James's spine as the name echoed quietly within him—Richard Morton.

Morton's face emerged in vivid detail among the murky remnants of the pub's décor: sharp angles, a self-satisfied smirk, and hands not quite clean from a night at a charity gala. But it wasn't merely his presence; it was the disturbing specifics—rumors of an abandoned estate on Wokingham's outskirts where black SUVs, dark as secrets, slipped in and out at all hours. There, amidst the crumbling facades and hidden basements, meetings took place that left behind more than just whispered deals: they found cryptic ledger entries, detailed records of illicit exchanges, and a series of eerie symbols—a single, unblinking eye enclosed in a circle—carved into hidden ledgers and scrawled in faded notebooks. It was the same sigil that had tormented Sarah in her final days, a trail of evidence that now wove a tangible pattern of systematic horror.

As Dave's heavy hand landed on his arm, pulling him back to the grim present, James found himself caught between the recollection of unspeakable details and the pervasive paranoia that gripped him. The inn, once a comfortable sanctuary, now seemed to conspire with their enemies—a gathering ground for secrets and a silent witness to every suspect move.

Even as the chatter of suspicious regulars and the clink of ill-fated glasses filled the air, James's thoughts remained fixated on the disturbing trail ahead. "Where did you drift off to?" Dave's voice was low, laced with anxious caution as he noted the far-off look in James's eyes. "It felt like you were lost in memories of a place long buried."

With a rueful smile reminiscent of old ghosts, James replied, "More than twenty-five years ago... back when everything started with Sarah." He took a deep, shuddering pull from his pint, feeling the bitterness of hops mingle with a taste of burnt hope. When he spoke again, his tone was grim, conspiratorial only shared with Dave.

"I think I know where to find answers," he declared, leaning deliberately close. "There's an old, forsaken estate past the town limits. Morton's been there more often than we'd like to believe. And he isn't alone. It's where they meet, where they trade in lives and secrets. I found a hidden ledger that details their operations —names, dates, transactions, and even a list of potential victims. Dave, this isn't just a meeting spot; it's their command post."

Dave's eyes widened, terror flickering in them like a warning light. "James, you can't go digging on your own, not now. Every step in that direction, every scrap of evidence you uncover, puts you directly in their crosshairs." His voice trembled, laden with a dread that cut through the murmur of conspiracies in every corner of Wokingham.

"I've no choice," James insisted, desperation sharpening his tone. "I'm closer than ever to the truth—closer than twenty-five years back. I owe it to Sarah, and I owe it to every soul this town has quietly bled." The inn around them seemed to breathe in his conviction, its tainted walls echoing his determination.

After a heavy, silent pause that spoke of shared history and peril, Dave exhaled a resigned breath, slumping his shoulders as if the weight of their collective burden was now tangible. "Okay, but understand—you're not doing this alone. I'm with you. And it's not just Sarah's ghost we're chasing. It's every hidden sin in Wokingham's dark underbelly."

James opened his mouth to dissent, but Dave's firm shake of his head silenced him. "No arguments. I've watched you carry this solitary burden for too long. Now, we face it together."

A surge of mingled relief and raw resolve burst in James, his voice breaking through gritted teeth, "Then together, we do this." Their agreement was a silent pact as they both drained their pints, each gulp a bitter promise of retribution.

Standing up, James squeezed Dave's shoulder with a ferocity that betrayed his inner tempest. "Thank you," he uttered, voice thick with gratitude and grief. "For bearing this cross with me." Dave's grip was unyielding, a testament to shared loyalty—a light in this contaminated crucible of despair. "Always," he vowed, his tone a low murmur mingled with pain and determination.

As they stepped out into the merciless night, the sensation was uncanny—the whispering winds of Wokingham seemed to carry voices, as if the town itself was spying on them. Streetlights cast long, accusing shadows, and the ambient hum served as a reminder that no dark corner was free from watchful eyes.

Then, as if the very fabric of their investigation demanded further reckoning, a news alert flickered on Dave's battered cellphone. In that brief, flashing moment, the magnitude of their enemy was laid bare—a new message revealed that another victim, bearing a striking resemblance to Sarah, had been found abandoned at the very estate James was about to investigate. Detailed forensic reports mentioned a chilling connection: a series of micro-filaments from a rare fiber, traced directly back to Morton's exclusive tailor.

A cold fury set both men ablaze. It was more than an isolated tragedy—it was a systematic, meticulously orchestrated massacre. And as the haunting strains of Radiohead's "Karma Police" seeped through the night's veil, a new realization crystallized: Wokingham, with all its whispered secrets and shadowed figures, was not merely a backdrop—it was an active, seething conspirator.

James Thornton's eyes ignited with a renewed, dangerous fire. He and Dave, united by a shared, perilous mission, marched toward the looming, sinister estate. Their purpose was no longer just to avenge Sarah; it was to dismantle a corrupt empire that had long terrorized the innocents of their town.

In that explosive moment of revelation, the stakes were unmistakably higher—corrupt power that spanned beyond personal vendettas and threatened to consume them all. With nothing left to lose and the fate of Wokingham hanging in the balance, they stepped into the abyss, resolved to bring down a force that thought itself untouchable.

CHAPTER 13: 'GIRLS & BOYS' (1999)

The Wokingham police station loomed like a sentient, predatory structure over James as he sat in his car, a brooding sentinel of faded power. Its red brick façade didn't stand for justice tonight; it mocked him with memories of endless days spent fighting within its confines, days that now twisted into a psychological trap from which escape seemed impossible. Every window and corner whispered betrayal, and the echoes of past courtrooms haunted him, turning what was once a proud symbol of law into a prison of suspicion and decay.

With a sigh that felt heavier than the chill in the air, James switched off the engine and gripped the door handle as though it were the last tether to hope. The previous night played over and over in his mind— the secretive gathering at The Ship, Dave's half-confessed words about an abandoned estate, and the shattered fragments of Sarah's final moments. The closer he felt to the truth, the more the looming specter of conspiracy within the department pressed against him. The Wokingham CID, it seemed, was steeped in corruption, its every shadow hiding complicity. Before he could expose those who had stolen Sarah's future, he needed to brave their twisted labyrinth.

James stepped into the station, each footfall a descent deeper into a mental claustrophobia, where tension swirled like a malignant fog. His secret investigation was the subject of wary glances and muted whispers among his colleagues—a silent consensus of fear and betrayal. The building itself seemed to be conspiring against him, a malignant force that transformed every corridor into a snare for the unwary.

Turning a corner, his eyes fell upon his desk—a solitary, chaotic island amid a sea of sidelong looks and veiled hostility. Files and coffee cups littered the surface, yet one paper stood out like a grave warning. As he approached, his pulse pounded in time with the thud of his dreading heart. The official letterhead bore the unmistakable mark of the department's high command—the cold, unyielding signature of Chief Superintendent Harris. It was a summons, a threat cloaked in bureaucratic language, aimed at reining in his unauthorized probing.

"Detective Sergeant Thornton,

Your presence is required in DI Grant's office at 9:00 AM sharp. A matter of some urgency has arisen regarding your current caseload and extracurricular activities. Failure to comply will result in immediate disciplinary action.

Chief Superintendent John Harris"

The words shattered him. Grant had betrayed him, using the department's conspiratorial machinery to muzzle an inconvenient truth. The station, a psychological prison built of trust and deceit, now squeezed him as guilt and unyielding resolve warred inside him. Rage exploded through him—how dare they try to silence his quest for truth, to bury the memory of Sarah as though her murder were nothing more than an administrative error?

Furious, he crumpled the paper in his clenched fist. His defiance burned with the promise of retribution as he marched toward

Grant's office, determined to confront the traitor who saw Sarah's demise as collateral damage. But then, a soft cough sliced through his storm of anger.

"James," came a whisper, urgent and tremulous. He whipped around to find DS Alice Delaney standing there, her usually composed features marred by tension. Her eyes, fierce yet haunted, betrayed layers of guilt and hidden motivations. Alice had long been a loyal partner, yet now her presence stirred a turbulent mix of trust and suspicion within him. Was she driven by a desire for redemption, or had she become another instrument of the covert conspiracy?

"Not now, Alice," James growled, shoving the reprimand paper deep into his pocket. "I have a meeting with Grant."

But before he could brush past her, Alice seized his wrist with a desperate firmness. "James, listen to me. I know what you're doing —what you're investigating." Her tone was edged with both fear and determination. He stiffened, anger and betrayal mingling as he glared at her hand gripping his. "I don't know what you're talking about," he snapped.

"Don't lie to me," she countered, her eyes pleading and defiant. "I know the truth, James. I can help you." In a split-second decision, she scanned the oppressive, conspiratorial space around them. Then, as though forced by a destiny steeped in regret and rebellion, she dragged him toward her unmarked car and practically shoved him inside. The door slammed, and with a screeching flurry of tires, they became fugitives from the psychological snare of the station, speeding away into the cold night.

The drive was charged with silence and unspoken confessions, the city's dark past receding behind them as they left Wokingham for the secluded countryside. Finally, on a lonely stretch of winding road beneath sallow streetlights, Alice broke the silence in a voice barely above a whisper. "I know about Sarah, James. I know you haven't stopped chasing the truth." Her confession resonated with more than just professional camaraderie—it carried the weight of personal loss and the burden of past failures.

James, his throat tight with a raw blend of grief and burning anger, turned away to stare at the fleeting landscape. "Then you understand why I can't let this go. Why I have to keep fighting." His words were drenched in sorrow for Sarah and a steely resolve for justice.

Alice's gaze softened for a moment before hardening once again. "I do understand. But you have to be careful. Grant and the higher-ups, with all their hidden agendas, won't let you trample into their trap. They'll not only shut you down—they'll obliterate you."

A bitter laugh, raw with despair and fury, rumbled from James. "They can try," he spat, fists clenching in defiance. "I won't stop— not until I've found every piece of the jigsaw and punished them for what they did to her."

The car slowed as they turned onto a narrow dirt track, the air thick with the scent of pine and decay—a portent of the darkness awaiting them. Alice met his eyes with a determined fire, her voice resolute and layered with remorse. "I want to help you. I've been lying about who I really am. For too long, I hid behind the uniform, scared of dissent, but I loved her too, James. I loved Sarah, and I know I failed her. I failed you. I couldn't bear to see the rot any longer." Her admission was raw, laden with personal torment and the desire to be complicit in rewriting the rules.

James searched her eyes and saw not deceit but a complex mosaic of guilt, love, and rebellion. "What are you saying?" he asked, his voice trembling with cautious hope.

"I'm saying I'm done being a good little soldier in a corrupt army," Alice declared, her tone both tender and unyielding. "I want to help bring those bastards to justice."

Her determined confession cemented the unspoken bond between them, forging an alliance born of loss and a shared hunger for truth. Slipping a slip of paper into his hand—a hastily gathered clue—she revealed, "I did some digging. There's an abandoned estate, fifteen miles outside town. It once belonged to the Hargrove family, before their fortunes crumbled. But there's been strange activity there lately: cars arriving at odd hours, lights burning in empty windows. I believe it connects directly to Sarah's murder."

As James scanned the hastily scribbled address, the fragments of a hidden conspiracy clicked together. Not only did the estate serve as a meeting point for shadowy figures, but it also whispered dark secrets about Sarah's case—a nexus where her death and the department's deepest lies converged.

"That's it," he murmured with grim realization. "That's where they hide, where all their secrets fester."

Alice's eyes hardened into cold resolve. "Then that's where we descend into darkness," she stated deliberately, as if her words carried the irrevocable weight of damnation. "We infiltrate quietly, peel back their layers of deceit, and expose their sins.

We're not just pursuing a case—we're entering the belly of the beast."

The finality of her words resonated as they clasped hands in the dim light—a silent promise fueled by vengeance, burdened by guilt, and shadowed by the specter of Sarah.

For the first time in years, a heavy yet earnest determination lifted James's spirit. For Sarah, for himself, and for all the others betrayed by the corrupt institution, he would dismantle every layer of deception. The journey ahead was perilous—a plunge into a darkness so deep it threatened to consume them both. Yet as the car sped down those winding lanes, the echo of Blur's "Girls & Boys" mingling with the thrum of his racing heartbeat, James Thornton knew one truth above all: the reckoning had begun, and there would be no mercy.

Only a descent into the heart of that darkness would deliver justice—cold, unflinching, and relentless.

CHAPTER 14: 'END OF A CENTURY' (PRESENT DAY)

The early morning light bled in slowly, a dull, lifeless grey that crept into James's cramped, disheveled kitchen—a mirror to his fractured inner state. Every weak beam fractured the room into baroque shadows sprawled across the cluttered table, strewn with a chaotic jumble of papers and scuffed-up, empty coffee cups. There he was, hunched over the mess as if his own despair were spilling into every corner, his eyes raw and marred by sleepless torment. Time had lost meaning in his frenzied quest—a desperate plunge into answers, justice, anything to counterbalance the void left by Sarah's brutal, senseless end.

An abandoned styrofoam cup lay like a forgotten relic by his elbow, its once-warm brew now a cold, bitter echo of his fading resolve. Even the adrenaline of caffeine pulsing through his veins couldn't burn away the deep, gnawing exhaustion—the silent testament to the unbearable weight of his own ruined soul.

Running a trembling hand over his stubbled jaw, James forced his scattered thoughts into a semblance of focus on the shreds of evidence sprawled before him. They were fragments of a mystery that mirrored his own shattered psyche: the desolate, abandoned estate, murky clandestine council meetings, and a web of corruption woven from greed and lies that had dragged Sarah into oblivion. It all sprawled before him in harsh, unforgiving black and white—jagged puzzle pieces that threatened to fracture further under the pressure of his relentless pursuit.

Yet, every revelation seemed to bleed into gaping voids, unanswered questions that gnawed at him like vermin in dark corners. Who was orchestrating this sprawling deception? What sins were they so desperate to silence, even if the cost was another life?

His mind was haunted by the memory of a frantic note found at the estate—a desperate scrawl that seared itself into his thoughts. "They're watching. Don't trust anyone." The words echoed, a ceaseless dirge against his inner vulnerabilities, as if warning him that every step deeper carried him closer to the edge of damnation. One miscalculated move, one wrong breath, and he feared he might end up cold and lifeless, just another casualty of the malignant storm that had swept Sarah away.

A sudden buzz from his mobile shattered his tortured reverie, his heart lurching against his ribs. With hesitating urgency, he answered the call from an unknown number.

"Thornton," he rasped, his voice cracked from years of insomnia and too many bitter cups of coffee.

There was a pregnant pause before a tentative, quivering voice emerged. "Detective Sergeant Thornton? It's Helen. Helen Matthews."

At the sound of her name, something stirred in him—a brief, flickering reprieve from the crushing fog of his mind. "Helen," he murmured, softening his tone ever so slightly, "what can I do for you?"

After another heavy pause punctuated by the familiar crackle of static, she spoke again, her voice thick with a palpable sorrow. "I found something, James. Amid Sarah's things. I think... you need to see it."

A surge of adrenaline propelled him upright. Grabbing his coat, he clutched the phone as if it were a lifeline. "Where are you?"

"At home," she whispered, her voice trembling as if in a ghostly half-light. "Please, James. Come quickly."

"On my way," he replied without hesitation, storming out into the day—a man half consumed by his own internal conflict, every step weighed down by the burden of his fractured purpose.

The drive to Helen's home blurred into a surreal procession of winding streets and flickering thoughts. His mind, as unsettled as ever, whirled through grim possibilities: could it be a diary? A coded letter? Some final, damning clue left behind by Sarah in a desperate act of resistance?

He barely recalled locking his car before he ascended the steps to her door. It swung open, not with the invitation of a familiar refuge, but rather with an unsettling, almost spectral welcome. Helen stood there, her face ghostly in its pallor, tear-streaked eyes emerging from beneath the veiling gloom that clung to her like a shroud.

"James," she whispered, her voice a fragile, broken lament heavy with pain, fear, and an unspoken dread. Her silent gesture beckoned him inside—a reluctant guide through a house that, under freshly sharpened perception, no longer exuded comforting normalcy but a subtle, oppressive menace, as if the walls themselves harbored dark secrets waiting to be unleashed.

Inside, the home retained the trappings of quaint English domesticity—floral prints and soft pastels—but there lingered an unnerving stillness. Every familiar corner seemed tainted by an unseen presence, and the quiet was laced with an expectation of impending calamity.

Helen led him into a dimly lit sitting room, her hands clasped tightly as though trying to ward off the malevolent spirits creeping through every silent crevice. Stopping abruptly beside an aged coffee table, her narrowed eyes fixated on a small, leatherbound book that lay on the surface like a damning indictment.

"I was sifting through Sarah's old belongings," she began, her voice distant and muffled, as though struggling to reclaim words from an abyss. "Things I couldn't face before... And I found... this."

Her shaking fingers extended the book toward him. With a heavy heart, James accepted it, a visceral knot forming in his gut as he brushed his skin against the supple, worn leather. The gilt edges whispered of faded grandeur as he slowly opened it, the sight of Sarah's unmistakable, flowing handwriting sending a shudder rippling down his spine.

This journal was not merely a record; it was a raw, searing slice of Sarah's last desperate moments, penned just weeks before her untimely demise. As he turned the fragile pages, fragments of horrifying revelations leaped out at him, embedding themselves in his mind with the force of physical blows.

"...secret council meetings held in the dead hours... something called The Circle... I'm being followed..."

Each word was a dagger, driving reality into his already splintered psyche. Then, his eyes froze on a name, twice underlined in bold, trembling strokes—the name that ignited a dark storm in his soul.

Richard Morton.

Morton, the notoriously treacherous property developer with a silver-tongued smile that masked a soul of icy cruelty, was not merely a name but the lynchpin of the conspiracy that festered at the heart of this grotesque tapestry. Everything—the forsaken estate, the clandestine meetings, the insidious corruption that had condemned Sarah—began to converge around him like a swirling vortex of greed and malevolence.

James's eyes met Helen's. In them he saw the reflection of his own dawning horror, mingled with heartbreak and a precursor to the abyss that awaited him. "Did you read this?" he rasped, his voice a blend of despair and grim determination.

She shook her head, vehemently, fresh tears cascading over her features. "I couldn't," she choked out, haunted by the invasive intimacy of the revelation. "It felt like invading her soul. But I knew... I knew you had to see it."

Gratitude warred with overwhelming grief as a heavy burden settled over him—a burden rescued from death's door, yet tethered to his own inevitable fate. For Sarah, for the hope that had vanished with her light, he absorbed the weight of that journal as if it were his own condemnation, each page an epitaph of a crumbling future.

Tenderly, yet with steel in his resolve, James slid the journal into his coat pocket, its oppressive heft an anchor dragging on his heart. His gaze hardened into a blaze of determination as he murmured, "Thank you... for trusting me with her truth."

Helen's smile was fleeting, her hands fluttering in visible tremors like caged birds desperate for escape. "All I want is the truth, James," she pleaded, voice raw with both hope and terror. "I need someone to make those monsters pay."

James's jaw contracted in grim acknowledgment—a silent vow as heavy as the darkness pooling beneath his eyes. "They will, Helen. I promise. I won't rest until every last culprit is dragged into the light, until they all atone for their sins."

In that charged moment, as he briefly squeezed her shoulder in a desperate bid to offer solace, he turned on his heel and strode from the oppressive confines of that subtle, menacing domicile. Every step radiated the tremors of a man who was not just chasing justice, but hurtling headlong into his own self-destruction—a sacrifice on the altar of a lost future.

Outside, the streets began their slow, indifferent awakening as the feeble sun battled the retreating shadows. Yet James was oblivious to the cadence of a new day; his mind roiled with dark possibilities. Morton. The Circle. Sarah's final, blood-soaked warnings. Every revelation wove itself into a grotesque tableau of impending doom—a puzzle with each piece a stitch in the tapestry of his collapsing sanity.

He slid into his car, seizing the steering wheel like a lifeline, his knuckles white in the dim morning light. Now, every lead was not a promise of retribution, but a beacon guiding him into the heart of darkness. The abandoned estate, the forbidden council records, and that brutal journal—a weapon forged in sorrow and foreboding—formed the battleground for his desperate crusade.

He would confront Morton first—the epitome of twisted power. That sly, venomous man, whose every smile concealed a lethal conspiracy, would be the first domino to fall. And if words or confrontations failed, James knew too well that his own hands would not shirk from the brutal task at hand. It was as if, in pursuing justice, he were willingly stepping into the maw of his own oblivion.

The Escort engine roared to life as Blur's "End of a Century" shattered the heavy silence, its pulsating rhythm merging with the pounding of his fractured heart. Cranking up the volume, the relentless beat coursing through his veins felt less like salvation and more like the ticking of a death knell—a vivid reminder that every step he took heralded his descent into the very darkness he aimed to vanquish.

He was almost at the edge. So tantalizingly close to a revelation that smelled of long-awaited justice, yet every step forward was a step toward his own final undoing. Each turn of the wheel, every lead pursued, felt inexorably like signing his own death warrant.

For Sarah—whose radiant presence had been extinguished by an unholy conjunction of greed, cruelty, and insatiable malevolence —James wasn't just fighting to bring perpetrators to justice. He was wading into a maelstrom, into a deadly pact that might consume him entirely. The lies, the secrets, the festering corruption at the core of Wokingham—they would all pay. And any soul foolish enough to stand against him would be dragged into the violent reckoning of his personal doomsday.

James's grip tightened on the steering wheel, resolute yet tremulous, as he steered himself into the darkness with the grim acceptance that his crusade was less about delivering justice and more an embrace of his own inevitable doom.

CHAPTER 15: 'LIVE FOREVER' (1999)

The wind lashed at James's threadbare jacket with a cruelty that seemed to mock his every step. Each hesitant footfall across the town square was a battle against an unseen, oppressive force —a force that sought to keep him from uncovering the vile truths embedded in his community. Overhead, the leaden sky and unyielding drizzle conspired with the atmosphere to mourn the festering rot of secrets, lies, and backroom deals that seeped from every crevice of Wokingham.

His gaze fixed on the council building at the far end of the square —a monstrous, corrupt edifice whose crumbling stone façade loomed like the grim embodiment of institutional decay and sin. Every etched scar in its weathered walls echoed the dark history of bribery, whispered threats, and the ruthless exploitation of the powerless. As James advanced, the building seemed to pulse with a malevolent energy, challenging him to confront the festering corruption hidden behind its ancient doors.

With his jaw clenched and hands buried deep in his pockets, James quickened his pace. Fury coiled within him, hot and acrid— a seething compulsion, not mere choice, to shatter the oppressive tyranny that had taken everything from him. Every muscle and thought urged him to storm the council building, to unleash his wrath on those immersed in a culture of impunity. Yet he knew that a direct assault would be futile; the powerful individuals exulting behind closed chambers were shielded by alliances and secrets. Even so, an internal compulsion—almost a madness fueled by guilt, isolation, and the desperate need for justice— drove him onward, isolating him further from any potential allies in a town where every friend had slowly receded into silence.

He turned away from the vile institution and headed to The Ship Inn, where the familiar green door promised a brief respite from the crushing weight of his quest. Inside, the smell of coffee and fried fare enveloped him like a temporary sanctuary, quelling the chill that had embedded itself deep within his bones. However, beneath this brief moment of reprieve lay a tension that interwove the pub's atmosphere with the investigation he was compelled to pursue—a tangled web where every friendly smile could hide a secret or an ulterior motive.

"Well, well, well...look who's graced us with their presence!" boomed Dave's voice from behind the bar. His large frame moved with practiced ease, yet today his demeanor betrayed deeper sorrows; the casual shrug of a stained tea towel and the familiar glint in his eyes carried the weight of unspoken guilt—a hint that past misdeeds and back-alley compromises had left their mark on him. His broad smile tried to mask the remorse of involvement in unsavory deals, deals that now linked directly to the corruption James was investigating.

"Morning, Dave," James replied, his voice fatigued, a grimace forced into a semblance of a smile. Slumping onto a worn stool, he ordered a pint of the finest ale. Dave's eyebrow arched skeptically as he retrieved the drink, and in that fleeting gesture, the layers of complicity and regret within him surfaced. Foam spilled over the bar, a minor uncontrolled detail amid the torrent of unspoken confessions.

"Bit early for that, innit?" Dave joked, but his eyes—darkened with the burden of shared guilt—flickered with a deeper understanding. With a lowered voice meant exclusively for James, he inquired, "This about that Cooke girl, isn't it? Sarah?" His tone suggested that not only was Sarah's fate intertwined with James's investigation, but that his own history might be entangled with those responsible for her suffering.

The question struck like a physical blow. James tightened his hold on the glass until his knuckles whitened, rage and grief battling within his constricted chest. "Yeah," he rasped through clenched teeth, his voice raw with suppressed torment. "It's about her." He could not bear how plainly the mention of Sarah dredged up both his personal heartache and the collective sins festering in the council's secret corridors.

Dave's expression softened, mixed with regret and a trace of fear. "It's been months," he ventured carefully, "perhaps it's time to let go... to move on?" But James's scorn was immediate, bitter as he slammed his fist against the worn wood of the bar. "Let go?" he thundered. "How can I ever let go when they stole everything from her? When they tore her from this world without a second thought?"

The pub seemed to grow quieter as his voice, trembling with raw emotion, filled the space with a palpable drive. There was no mere anger here—it was a compulsion, etched into his soul, that would not permit him to rest until every corrupted official, every conspirator, faced retribution. "I'll never allow them to escape justice," he growled, eyes ablaze with a fervor that bordered on madness. "I'll hunt every last one of those monsters down and make them pay—pay for what they did, for what they stole from us."

Dave's hand landed on his shoulder in a gesture that was both paternal and laden with his own regret. "Listen, lad," he cautioned, his voice gravelly with experience and guilt. "You're playing a dangerous game. These people won't hesitate to obliterate you if you defy them." The quiet gravitas of his tone revealed memories of compromises made in darkened backrooms—compromises that now haunted both of them.

A laugh, both derisive and desperate, escaped James as he shook off Dave's attempt at restraint. "I know exactly who I'm dealing with," he spat. "They killed Sarah because she was too close to their secrets. I won't stop until every shadow of their misdeeds is dragged into the light." His voice cracked, tears finally betraying the quiet desperation of a man compelled by forces beyond mere choice. The controlled madness in his eyes was a testament to how isolated he had become—a lone crusader in a town that systematically abandoned him.

"They tortured her," James choked out through sobs, his body trembling. "They stripped her of everything until nothing was left but a shattered shell, and then—then they tore her away from me with a cruelty that defies belief." Dave's face softened even further, a mixture of sorrow and remorse; he knew too well the devastating cost of engaging with these dark powers—a truth he had fought against and, in quieter moments, even been complicit in.

"I'll make them pay," James vowed, his voice barely above a whisper yet fierce with the compulsion that drove him. "Even if it costs me every part of what I have left."

Dave's hand returned to his shoulder, this time offering a semblance of solace despite the heavy undercurrent of his own conflicted past. "I believe you, lad," he murmured, his map of personal failures and hard-won lessons etched in every line of his face. "But remember, revenge is a path with no return. Once you step onto it, you can never escape its pull." His words connected the pub table directly to the ongoing investigation, as if hinting that the web of corruption that had ensnared Sarah was now tightening around both of them.

Meeting Dave's eyes, James acknowledged that their shared determination was born not merely of choice but of a psychological compulsion—an unyielding need for retribution that isolated him from the few legitimate allies he once had. "You don't have to face this alone, James," Dave continued, his voice deep and laden with his own demons of guilt. "There are others who loved Sarah, others who want justice as much as you do. We're all caught in the same vise grip—justice for Sarah is a battle for us all." Amidst the rekindled hope, James could no longer ignore that in his obsessive quest, he had grown fundamentally isolated, left to fight a war that claimed him piece by piece from the inside.

A lump seized his throat as he managed a hoarse, "Thank you." In that moment, amid the swirling scents and murmurs of the pub, he realized that this pursuit was not merely a calculated mission —but a compulsive drive that had taken hold of him, leaving behind a trail of forsaken allies and a mind consumed by relentless obsession.

Dave's crooked smile, tinged with the bitter residue of his own past missteps, offered a final reassurance. "That's what friends are for," he said quietly, a lifeline amid the storm, "We'll navigate this darkness together, and we'll make sure Sarah's death means something."

As James raised his glass and clinked it against Dave's, the amber liquid shimmered like a beacon of resolve and shared burden. In that fragile moment, the ale was more than a drink—it was a distilled promise of courage against the corruption that had tainted their town, an emblem of the psychological compulsion that drove him to seek justice.

James drank deeply, letting the bitter hops and sweet malt invigorate the resolve that had morphed into something uncontrollable—a necessity for redemption and a refusal to be swallowed by the relentless isolation. Each swallow reaffirmed his oath: to expose the truth, dismantle the malignant power of that council building, and exact a reckoning upon those who had shattered Sarah's world.

Setting his empty glass down, his jaw steeled with grim determination, James knew the path ahead would be fraught with treacherous sacrifices. Yet, even as the shadow of isolation deepened around him, he embraced this destiny—not as a choice, but as an inescapable compulsion forged in pain and a haunted past.

For Sarah. For the bright soul that had once lit his darkened world. For the hope that even amidst overwhelming corruption and solitude, justice would prevail.

James Thornton refused to hide any longer. He refused to run, to let the shadows win. Tonight, under a bruised sky that bore silent witness, he vowed to stand and fight, becoming the instrument of retribution Sarah deserved.

And may God help those who dared oppose him—as he set his eyes on the night sky and almost heard Sarah's whisper urging him forward, a spectral promise that together, even the most isolated and broken could bring light back into a world mired in darkness.

CHAPTER 16: 'LUCKY MAN' (PRESENT DAY)

The Ship Inn had transformed into a treacherous arena, its once-comforting hum now replaced by the oppressive silence of calculated threat. James stood near the door, his pulse a relentless drumbeat in a cage of raw fear and defiance. Every shadow in the room seemed to whisper of betrayal and hidden peril. This was no safe retreat tonight—it was a crucible where past sins would be rehashed and futures shattered.

Throughout the day, anxiety had coiled around him like a venomous snake, and his mind had been tormented by the ceaseless repetition of damning evidence. Sarah's journal, its pages crumbling with the weight of unspeakable truths, lay heavy in his coat pocket—a ticking time bomb ready to expose the atrocity that had ruptured their lives. Failure was a specter he simply could not entertain.

As the minutes dragged on with excruciating slowness, a glance at his watch brought him face to face with the inevitable trio: Morton, Willis, and Hadley. These men were not mere adversaries but embodiments of institutional rot—Morton, the corrupt councilman whose arrogance was matched only by his ruthless ambition; Willis, whose jittery energy masked a cunning heart corrupted by power; and Hadley, the retired superintendent whose icy, calculated poise barely concealed an insatiable hunger for control. Their presence cast long, sinister shadows over the battleground that was the Ship Inn.

A creak at the door shattered James's inner maelstrom. Dave, the pub owner and an unlikely guardian in this psychological warzone, emerged from behind the counter. His expression was etched with a concern that reached into the depths of James's frayed nerves as he crossed the room, placing a reassuring yet determined hand on his shoulder.

"Everything all right, lad?" Dave murmured, his voice low, as if trying to stave off the encroaching menace. "You look like you're facing a firing squad."

James offered a self-mocking laugh that rang hollow in his ears. "Might as well be," he responded, his voice tight with a blend of grim resolve and barely concealed terror. "These bastards aren't going down without a fight. They'll do whatever it takes to choke the truth."

Dave's grip tightened, and his eyes flashed with steeled determination. "Let them try," he growled. "We have something they'll never possess—the uncompromising force of truth and justice."

Swallowing hard, James felt the bile rise in his throat. He was painfully aware of the mortal danger closing in around him. Despite the peril, he clutched Dave's forearm in gratitude. "Thank you. I couldn't face this without you," he rasped.

Dave's smile was a grim slash against the dim light. "Yes, you could have, but you're a good man, James Thornton. A brave one. Don't ever forget that," he insisted.

Before James could muster another word, the pub's door flung open, spilling a gust of cold darkness into the charged air. Richard Morton entered like a predator eyeing its prey, his coat billowing dramatically—a theatrical veneer masking the soul of a man who thrived on power and cruelty. Pausing at the threshold, his eyes locked onto James, and his lips curled into a sneer laced with disdain.

"Sergeant Thornton," Morton drawled with a chilling calm, the very sound a calculated provocation. "I trust your visit is of utmost importance, though I doubt it will disturb my busy schedule."

Unyielding, James met his gaze, his own eyes blazing with a storm of anger and dread. "Sit down, Councillor," he commanded, gesturing toward a booth in the darkest corner of the room—a designated place for inevitable showdown. "We'll speak once your cronies arrive."

Morton's feigned surprise gave way to a mocking bow as he coerced himself to the booth, slotting into a role of arrogant menace beside Willis. The sight only twisted the knot of anxiety in James's gut tighter, every step toward conflict weighing on him like an executioner's block.

Moments later, Henry Willis burst in with wild, disheveled hair and a flushed, almost panicked countenance, his eyes betraying both cunning and desperate self-preservation. He barely acknowledged James before joining Morton; their rapid, whispered collusion was a staccato prelude to inevitable doom. Each word they exchanged was like a bullet aimed not just at James, but at his very soul.

Unwavering despite the psychic assault, James's voice was low and tremulous with a mix of fury and resigned suffering. "I've seen the depths of this darkness, lived surrounded by it ever since you ripped Sarah away from us. There's nothing you can inflict on me that hasn't already scarred me."

Then came George Hadley, the final piece of this grim triumvirate. The retired superintendent moved in with an air of sinister superiority, every measured step and cool glance dripping with cold calculation. He removed his gloves with deliberate precision, a ritual of control over chaos, and folded them as if sealing away a dark secret.

"Well, well," Hadley drawled in a tone heavy with condescension, his gaze slicing through the tense air. "The gang is assembled. What brings you here, Sergeant?"

James did not permit Hadley the satisfaction of his mockery. With deliberate resolve and mounting desperation, he closed the battered distance between them and sat opposite the three conspirators. The oppressive silence of the inn pulsed with barely-contained violence as he extracted Sarah's journal from his coat, slamming it onto the scarred table. "It's time we talked about Sarah Matthews," he proclaimed, his voice a measured storm of controlled rage and palpable terror.

Morton's face turned ashen, Willis emitted a strangled, nervous hiss, while Hadley maintained his icy demeanor, his eyes meeting James's with deliberate calculation. "I'm at a loss for your delusions, Sergeant," Hadley said smoothly, fingers steepled in an artful display of false calm. "Any allegations you make are baseless. Miss Matthews's death was nothing more than a tragic accident."

"Bullshit," James spat, leaning in as if to impose his very will upon them. "Sarah was murdered, and I have the evidence that ties you three to it."

Willis's head shook in silent panic while Morton subtly kicked him under the table—a silent order to shut up. Morton's glare sharpened into a weaponized smile as he faced James, but there was a vacancy there, a hollow mask over his true, ruthless nature.

"I have records, call logs, and twisted correspondences that prove your meetings and your threats were all orchestrated when Sarah got too close to uncovering the truth," James continued, his finger drumming the journal's beat as if marking an execution countdown.

For a fleeting moment, Hadley's veneer faltered, a tremor shadowing his eyes before he marshaled his composure. "Your bluff won't hold up in a court of law, Sergeant," he sneered, the slight quaver betraying his inner turmoil. "Those scribbles could be interpreted in a thousand ways."

James's lips curled into a bitter smile, devoid of any warmth. "Maybe not in a courtroom," he conceded, voice low and lethal, "but in the court of public opinion? When I unveil your underhanded deals and exposed misdeeds to every corner of Wokingham, your reputations will crumble. The people will devour you, tear you limb from limb, and scatter your remains to the vultures. And I will witness every moment, knowing that justice, long delayed, is finally served."

As his words reverberated like the toll of a death knell, a paralyzing silence descended. Anger, fear, and raw resentment danced in the eyes of his adversaries before Morton finally snarled, "You're making a grave mistake, Thornton. You have no idea how deep we're willing to sink to protect our interests."

With the sudden force of a wild animal, Morton stood, the scraping of his chair echoing ominously. "I'm not leaving," he declared, voice low and resolute. "I'll see this through at any cost— be it for Sarah, for Wokingham, or for every decent soul trampled under our boots." His eyes, burning with a dangerous intensity, swept over his cohorts and then back at James. "I suggest you begin your final reckoning, gentlemen. The time has come, and every sin will demand its due."

In that charged moment, as the inn became a psychological battlefield where every glance and heartbeat was loaded with lethal promise, James felt himself teetering on the brink of irreversible transformation. He rose as if stiffened by resolve and terror in equal measure, clutching Sarah's journal to his chest like a talisman against the coming storm. With one last lingering look at the arena of his tormentors, he stepped out into the night, the cool air a bitter reminder of the path he had chosen—a path from which there was no turning back.

CHAPTER 17: WAKE UP BOO! (PRESENT DAY)

The dilapidated Hargrove Estate stood before them like a monstrous embodiment of Wokingham's festering corruption—a crumbling citadel whose decaying walls and invasive vines bore silent witness to decades of exploitation and deceit. Its once-grand facade, now a canvas of neglect and twisted ivy, seemed to leer at the trespassers as if it had absorbed every hidden sin of the town. James Thornton paused at the fringe of the encroaching wilderness that was once a manicured lawn, the dimming sun casting eerie, elongated shadows that mimicked the long reach of the estate's malefic influence. This was the very site where Sarah's life had been so cruelly snuffed out—a physical monument to the unchecked greed and systemic rot that had plagued these grounds for far too long.

Next to him, Alice Fletcher shifted with a restless anxiety, her hand trembling as it brushed the concealed pistol under her jacket. The autumn air was heavy with the decay of fallen leaves and the distant murmur of Wokingham's evening—the sounds of a town too accustomed to its hidden vices. "Are you certain we must press on, James?" she whispered, her eyes flitting around the oppressive perimeter of the estate. "Do we truly wish to rouse whatever malignant force resides here?"

James inhaled deeply, his voice resolute despite the icy dread that surged within him. "I must, Alice," he said, his tone a blend of conviction and anguish. "For Sarah, and for all those whose lives were shattered by this entrenched corruption. There's no retreat now—only the pursuit of a bitter truth."

Alice met his gaze, determination hardening her features as she prepared for the arduous path ahead. "Lead on—I'm right behind you."

Trailing in their wake was Willis Harper, their tech specialist, whose perpetual expression of apprehension and uncertainty belied a hardened resolve born of countless nights dissecting Sarah's investigation. Each piece of the puzzle had led them here— to this cursed estate, a grotesque monument to the very evil they had sworn to confront.

As they neared the massive oak doors, it seemed as though the entrance itself was a sentinel of guilt, its intricate carvings of twisting vines and all-seeing eyes an unblinking testament to The Circle's pervasive surveillance. James hesitated, his hand hesitating on the ornate, decay-ridden threshold. "Are you prepared for this?" he murmured over his shoulder, eyes catching Willis's. "Once we cross that line, there will be no turning back."

Willis swallowed, his voice barely audible. "I'm not ready," he confessed, his uncertainty laced with resignation. "But for Sarah —and for everyone caught in this rot—I must see it through."

For a long, charged moment, James scrutinized his companions, the flicker of fear mingling with steely resolve in their eyes. Satisfied they were as ready as fate would allow, he turned back to the foreboding doors. With a deep, shuddering push, he set them swinging inward, the ancient hinges groaning like the lamentations of a damned past. Inside, a grand foyer loomed in ghostly semi-darkness, where dust motes floated like memories of lives decayed by time. The air was pungent with neglect, and every step on the worn carpet echoed the loss of a once-splendid era.

They advanced cautiously through the corridors, each room a silent mausoleum of a corrupted legacy. Portraits of stern ancestors stared from fractured frames, their eyes heavy with accusation and remorse, following the intruders through halls stripped of their former opulence—a visceral reminder of the sins that had built this kingdom of deceit.

At the corridor's terminus, James's keen ears picked up a hushed murmur, barely audible behind a heavy oak door. He raised his hand, a silent command for Alice and Willis to pause. The murmur swelled into a murky chorus of voices, each note deepening the prickling dread that wound its way up their spines. Exchanging a look of grim resolve, they silently fanned out to flank the door. James's hand gripped the cold metal handle as he pressed it down slowly; the door creaked open with a reluctant protest, revealing a dimly lit study.

Inside, dark mahogany bookshelves loomed, burdened with the weight of dusty tomes and hidden records. Dominating the space was a massive oak table, cluttered with papers and exposed secrets. Around it sat the remaining members of The Circle —figures whose once-imposing authority had been blighted by insidious guilt and creeping despair. Councillor Ward's face, etched with lines of cunning and petty cruelty, relaxed into an expression of thinly veiled contempt; Richard Morton's eyes sparkled with a perverse delight, each glimmer hinting at the depths of his depravity; and the other dignitaries, embattled and weary, bore the marks of a conscience long corroded by power.

The moment the intruders breached their sanctum, the room's

atmosphere grew taut with alarm. Every head snapped toward them, eyes wide in frozen shock against the backdrop of oppressive silence—broken only intermittently by the rhythmic drip of water from a neglected ceiling.

In a sudden, explosive gesture, Councillor Ward leaped to his feet, his features contorting with thunderous anger. "What is the meaning of this?" he snarled, his voice a low, menacing rumble. "How dare you defile our meeting?"

Without missing a beat, James strode forward, his revolver a cold extension of his righteous resolve. "It's over, Ward," he declared, every word slicing through the stifling tension. "We've uncovered your corrupt circle—your intricate web of lies, manipulation, and betrayal. Your time is up."

Richard Morton let out a harsh, mocking laugh, his tone dripping with venom. "You really think you can crash in here and shatter what we've built, Thornton?" he sneered. "We are the pillars of this community—the very backbone that holds it together. Our influence spans far beyond your isolated little crusade."

James's grip on his weapon tightened as he replied steadily, "Maybe, but you've reached beyond your limit this time. We have this—evidence so damning it implicates every one of you in Sarah's murder. And I won't stop until every last one of you is held accountable."

Ward's fury deepened, his fists clenching as he spat out, "You have no idea the forces you're meddling with. The control we exercise goes beyond your wildest nightmares." With a sweeping, imperious gesture across the room, he continued, "We aren't some disorganized rabble, Thornton. We are the very foundation of this town—doctors, lawyers, politicians—bound by The Circle's insidious code. And we will not be overthrown by an upstart cop."

A chill ran down James's spine as he absorbed the weight of Ward's threat—the realization that he was confronting not merely corrupt officials, but a labyrinthine cabal whose tendrils reached out far beyond the crumbling walls of the estate. Yet, bolstered by Sarah's fractured memory—a mosaic of love, loss, and unyielding pain—James resolved to face this darkness head-on. Her remembrance was not a simple call for justice; it was a psychological anchor amid turbulent seas, a reminder of everything they had lost and might never fully reclaim.

Standing amidst the fraught standoff, James's gaze swept the room, meeting the haunted, conflicted eyes of each conspirator. "Your Circle, your power—none of it matters," he growled defiance. "All I care about is the truth—justice for Sarah, and for all the lives you've irreversibly tainted."

Ward's twisted snarl deepened as he leaned forward. "You dare threaten us, despite our legacy?" he hissed. "You know nothing of our true strength." His words pulsed with a malignant promise as he began to summon his cohorts, "This isn't your private vendetta, Thornton. We are the embodiment of Wokingham's might—and you are standing in our way."

The tension exploded into chaotic motion: chairs scraped, weapons were brandished, and paranoia electrified the stale air as members of The Circle scrambled to salvage their crumbling dominion. Amid the turmoil, James held his ground, his allies flanking him resolutely.

Then a crystalline command cut through the pandemonium—a

voice of unseasoned authority. "Stand down." Every eye turned to the far end of the table where Emerson, a tall, distinguished man whose countenance betrayed both regret and firm resolve, had risen. "There has been enough bloodshed."

Ward's eyes narrowed into a venomous glare at the sight of what he deemed a traitor. "Emerson, you treacherous turncoat," he spat, his tone laced with contempt. "How dare you—"

Emerson's voice sharpened, brooking no argument as he interjected, "Enough. This filth has stained us long enough. It is time to put an end to this cycle—once and for all." He paused, his gaze locking with James's, as if burdened by the weight of his own complicity. "Detective, you must understand—the Circle is finished. We are prepared to surrender all our evidence and cooperate fully with your investigation."

A charged silence fell. For a heartbeat, resistance pulsed in the charged air—a palpable hesitation that belied years of entrenched power. Emerson's words hung between defiance and desperation, as if surrender were not a triumph but a reluctant capitulation, an admission that the corrupt past might still cast long shadows over the uncertain future.

James's surprise was evident. "What do you mean?" he demanded, his mind whirling with skepticism and hidden doubts. "You expect me to simply let this be?"

Emerson raised a conciliatory hand, though his eyes betrayed an inner torment. "No, not merely let it go," he explained, his voice heavy with the sorrow of inevitable losses. "I'm saying that The Circle's era is at an end. The truth must emerge, and we must all face the consequences of our actions." His gaze hardened for a moment, the resolve intermingled with the fear that triumph might prove as corrosive as the sins they had committed.

For a long, charged moment that seemed to stretch into eternity, James studied Emerson—a man whose surrender was laced with both contrition and a hint of resignation. Finally, with visible reluctance, James lowered his weapon. "Fine," he murmured, his voice trembling with both relief and lingering mistrust. "I'll hold you to that promise, Emerson."

Emerson's nod was slow, weighed down by years of regret before he turned to his fellow conspirators. "Then let us begin."

With an uneasy air of finality, The Circle members began to assemble their incriminating files, their faces a mix of haunted resignation and bitter defiance. Alice stepped up beside James, her voice a blend of cautious hope and pragmatic suspicion. "Do you really believe he means it?" she whispered, eyes still darting about as if expecting betrayal at any moment.

James's gaze shifted back to Emerson, who now supervised the chaotic dismantling of his own criminal legacy. "I don't know," he admitted softly, the complexity of his emotions reflected in every weary line of his face. "But for Sarah—whose memory is as much a call to confront our personal demons as it is a plea for justice—we have no choice but to try."

Alice's determined nod bore the weight of a promise forged in despair. "Then let's do this. The sooner we dismantle these lies, the sooner Wokingham might begin to mend. Though I fear this victory may be as transient as a fleeting dawn."

Throughout the long, sleepless night, the trio combed through corridors of evidence and buried transactions like relics of a decayed regime. The study transformed into a war room under the flicker of a single lamp—a feeble light in a cavern of secrets. With every document, every shattered piece of the puzzle, James felt a conflicted solace mingled with a growing dread that perhaps, like the estate itself, this triumph was built on a foundation riddled with rot.

As morning crept over the estate and its grim legacy, they sat among scattered files, the first hesitant rays of sunlight fighting the pervasive gloom. James surveyed his team with a complex mix of triumph, exhaustion, and sorrow. "It's finished," he whispered, though his tone hinted that the battle against corruption was far from over.

Alice, leaning back with both pride and a trace of melancholy, said softly, "Sarah would have wanted this—but perhaps she never imagined the cost it would exact on us."

Willis exhaled slowly, as though releasing years of pent-up despair. "It may be over for tonight, but I fear we're merely peering over the edge of something even darker."

With a heavy heart and a lingering sense of foreboding, James rose, the burden of their success mingling with the uncertainty of what lay ahead. "Let's hope we can keep it this way," he muttered.

Together, they departed the estate—a battlefield that had mirrored the very blight of Wokingham's soul. As the fully risen sun cast its pale light on the desolation below and they glanced back at the crumbling fortress, James couldn't shake the feeling that the true fight was only just beginning, and that in the battle against corruption, victories might always be as hollow and transient as the memories they sought to honor.

CHAPTER 18: THERE SHE GOES (PRESENT DAY)

The days after the confrontation at the Hargrove Estate dissolved into a ceaseless procession of relentless tasks. James Thornton, Alice Fletcher, and Willis Harper moved determinedly through the once silent corridors, their every step unearthing another layer of long-hidden deceit that poisoned Wokingham. While each new discovery dismantled a piece of The Circle's empire, it also revealed how deeply its corruption had seeped into the town —a realization that left a lingering doubt in the back of every mind, as if the true rot might still be festering unseen.

Wokingham, with its picturesque settings nestled along the River Thames and its storied community spirit, had always appeared a haven of quiet charm. Yet beneath that gentle facade, fear and manipulation had long cast a pall over its streets. The revelation of The Circle's transgressions sent unsettling ripples through town life; even local haunts like The Ship Inn transformed into secretive enclaves where whispered conversations and furtive glances betrayed trepidation over the true extent of the damage done. The apparent victory brought with it not the sweet taste of liberation alone, but a bitter awareness that the abyss of corruption might never be fully closed.

Haunted by the heavy burden of responsibility, James navigated these turbulent times with a soul forever altered by his quest for justice. Memories of Sarah—her fierce dedication and the heart-wrenching circumstances of her demise—weighed on him more profoundly than any success could relieve. Wandering through Elms Field, the park in which dreams had once intertwined with whispered secrets over autumn-tinted leaves, he felt every rustle of the wind as a painful reminder of loss. "Nothing could ever replace you, Sarah," he murmured into the chill, the void she left transforming each recollection into a tender, unhealing ache. Even as evidence mounted and hope dared glimmer, every victory was tinged with the foreboding sense that no outcome could truly mend a fractured soul.

On a crisp and somber morning, James returned to The Ship Inn —a beleaguered sanctuary where faded lamplight met the damp autumn air. Inside, Alice and Willis were amid mountains of documents and photographs, each piece a key to unlocking The Circle's concealed malevolence.

"Morning, James," Alice greeted in a voice that was both steady and weary. "We've uncovered more evidence today."

Sliding into his customary seat at the corner table, James let the familiar aroma of ale and the subdued murmur of conversation flank him, even as he recognized that normalcy was now haunted by the shadows of his past. "Every shred counts," he answered softly.

Willis, his eyes reflecting exhaustion yet steeled with resolve, added, "I've been cross-referencing financial data with property records. There's a pattern here, one that suggests the corruption might extend deeper than we ever imagined."

Their painstaking cataloging of covert deals and backroom handshakes transformed the Hargrove Estate into the nerve center of their crusade—a monument to human greed and a staging ground for hard-won truth. With each revelation, the foundation of The Circle crumbled further, yet every new fact reminded them that victory might be as fragile as it was momentous.

Still, despite their progress, Sarah's absence was a constant, spectral presence. In quieter moments, her memory filled the spaces where hope had once flourished. James frequently found himself back at Elms Field, staring at the gnarled, weeping willow beneath which so many dreams had been shared. One cold, reflective twilight, as the sun bled vibrant shades of pink and orange into the dusky sky, he sat on that familiar bench. Carefully, he retrieved a worn photograph of Sarah—captured during happier times in her favorite garden—and whispered, "This is for you, Sarah." The soft strains of "There She Goes" by The La's carried his bittersweet lament, each note etching deeper into the man he had become—a man irrevocably scarred by loss and the price of truth.

At The Ship Inn, a stark transformation had taken hold. The space, now a gathering ground for unyielding determination amid palpable tension, brimmed with irrefutable evidence linking The Circle's remaining operatives to a trail of abject exploitation. Alice's careful presentation of financial records and Willis's digital reconstructions painted a damning picture, yet even this rigor could not fully dispel the thick, oppressive air that clung to them like a second skin.

"We can't miss a single detail," Alice stated firmly, her tone carrying both resolve and a mourning for the innocence lost to deception.

James acknowledged her words with a heavy nod—a silent pledge of commitment laced with profound sorrow. "Let's review it all once more."

Under the solitary glow of a single lamp, their makeshift war room—a repurposed study in the now-deteriorated Hargrove Estate—became a theater of shadows, where every movement and whispered strategy bore the weight of past sacrifices. With each new piece of the puzzle, James felt the cumulative pressure of the investigation transform him further; he was no longer the same man who had dared to dream in Elms Field. The journey had altered him irreparably, etching into his heart an enduring mix of determination, guilt, and uncertainty.

When the news of the Trial of the Century broke—a trial held in the repurposed halls of the once-glorious Hargrove Estate—the atmosphere in the courtroom was nothing short of oppressive. National media thronged Wokingham, their buzzing presence amplifying the relentless pressure within those walls. As James took his seat at the front, clutching Sarah's journal as both talisman and torment, the space seemed to constrict under an almost unbearable psychological weight. Every piece of evidence they presented was a double-edged sword—both a nail in the coffins of the corrupt and a reminder that the deeper, lingering corruption might never be fully exorcised.

James's opening statement resonated against the heavy, draconian atmosphere of the courtroom. His voice, clear yet trembling with unspoken grief, wove an intricate narrative of systemic deceit and abuse. As he recounted each hidden transaction and every coerced testimony, the oppressive air bore down on him like a judgment of its own—a constant reminder that every victory was steeped in the agony of irreversible change.

Opposite him, Councillor Ward and Richard Morton sat at the defense table, their formerly formidable air now reduced to brittle facades barely concealing the crumbling foundation beneath. "We've documented secret meetings, illicit transactions, and testimonies from those too frightened to speak," James declared, his words slicing through the stifling tension. Each witness that took the stand added a note to the symphony of condemnation, yet beneath it all, an eerie uncertainty lingered: Was The Circle truly vanquished, or had its poisonous influence merely retreated into hidden recesses?

In his final declaration, James proclaimed with a voice that rang out across the now oppressive silence, "The Circle's reign of terror must end here. Their actions have ravaged lives, and it is our duty to reclaim justice for every soul lost." Yet even as the foreperson's solemn pronouncement of guilt echoed around the room, a pervasive heaviness—an awareness that the corruption might still lurk in dim corners—hung over the proceedings. The victory tasted of both retribution and a lingering dread that some darkness might have only been forced to hide rather than altogether vanish.

Leaving the courtroom, James felt an ambiguous onslaught of relief and sorrow. The judgment, though legally conclusive, failed to exorcise the oppressive ghosts that had haunted him throughout the investigation. Outside, the cool evening air did little to dispel the inner chill that clung to him. The journey back through Elms Field was transformed into a pilgrimage of deep regret, where every shadow and rustling leaf recalled Sarah's smile —and the bitter promise that her sacrifice might have been in vain.

As he hesitated by the weathered park bench where Sarah's name was indelibly etched in stone, James whispered a hollow apology to the memory of promises lost. "I'm sorry," he murmured, recognizing that each step forward was weighted by both triumph and irrevocable loss. A bitter wind swept by, its sound a cold echo of a presence that once promised solace but now only reinforced his internal desolation.

Inside The Ship Inn, Alice and Willis mirrored his conflicted spirit. Their silent, shared understanding—an amalgam of hard-won victory and the ever-looming cost of their mission—was palpable. "We did it," Alice said softly, though every word was laced with the sorrow of what had transpired.

"But at what cost?" James replied, the question heavy on his soul, imbuing the running strains of "There She Goes" with an added nuance of despair. Even as the triumphant notes played, an unsettling ambiguity persisted about whether the corruption was truly vanquished or if its remnants would one day reemerge.

Later, alone in his flat, James stared into the darkness beyond his window as his thoughts circled inexorably back to Sarah's notebook—a repository of her hopes and haunting reflections. Instead of bringing comfort, a single quote from her work resonated like a painful echo. Every note of "There She Goes" reverberated through the sparse room, each lyric a stark reminder of the woman he had lost and the shattered person he had become. Clenching his jaw against a rush of tears, he snapped the notebook shut, determined not to let his grief shatter the fragile resolve that had carried him this far.

As dawn bled slowly into the horizon, James felt a bittersweet closure. The once suffocating shadows of Wokingham appeared to recede, replaced by the harsh glare of a new day that offered neither complete redemption nor the promise of absolute purity. On his balcony, he inhaled the crisp morning air—a fragile mixture of hope and lingering regret—and looked out over a town that stirred with cautious energy. The red post-boxes stood like silent sentinels, and the cobblestone streets gleamed under a light that belied the town's haunted past.

"There she goes," he whispered to the awakening day, a quiet homage to Sarah—a reminder that her memory would forever guide him through moments of both radiant hope and unyielding sorrow. With a gaze that was as determined as it was irreparably altered, James stepped into the uncertain morning light. Though his battle against corruption had delivered a decisive blow, the scars of the ordeal—and the ambiguous promise of true redemption—would accompany him forever.

Epilogue: Walkaway (Present Day)

The cemetery lay in a hushed state, the pale mist of dawn softening the sharp outlines of the headstones. James ambled along the winding path he knew so well, his footsteps muffled by the dewy grass. In his grasp, he cradled a lone white rose, its petals timidly unfurling to greet the day.

Sarah's resting place was unpretentious—a simple granite slab bearing her name and the dates that marked a life brutally truncated. Dropping to his knee, James gently placed the rose upon the stone, his reverence intermingled with sorrow.

"We got them, Sarah," he murmured, the tremor in his voice betraying a turbulent mix of grief and defiance. "Morton, Willis, Hadley... that vile crew. They'll answer for what they did to you.

For all of us."

A heavy swallow accompanied his blinking gaze, straining to hold back the cascade of tears. "But it's never enough. It's a mere beginning—a fragile hope for Wokingham to mend and perhaps evolve into something nobler than it once was."

A subtle breeze stirred his hair, mingling the scent of fresh earth with the promise of new beginnings. James shut his eyes, absorbing the quiet resurgence of hope. Though he doubted peace would ever fully be his again, this small solace was a tentative step toward healing—a glimmer as delicate and transient as the rose resting on Sarah's grave.

Rising slowly, he pressed his hand against the cool, unyielding granite. "I miss you," he whispered, each word heavy with the weight of remembrance. "Every damn day. Yet I swear, Sarah—I will honor you. I will keep fighting. For you. For everything you believed in."

With one final, resolute nod toward the woman who had transformed him, James straightened his back. The sun now crested the horizon, imbuing the sky with lavish streaks of gold and orange, while the serene melody of birdsong floated on the wind—a gentle punctuation to the silence of the cemetery.

James inhaled deeply, letting the air fill him with steady determination before turning away. The world was stirring, the first hints of daylight bearing witness to a new day. At long last, for the first time in what felt like endless struggles, he was ready to confront it head-on.

As he neared the towering gates, a familiar strain of music danced upon the breeze, summoning memories. Tilting his head, a soft smile touched his lips when he recognized the opening notes of "Walkaway" by Cast—a song entwined with the last twilight shared with Sarah, when they had both dared to dream of a future free from Wokingham's long shadows. Now it resonated as both a remembrance of what once was and a tentative pledge of what might yet come.

James hummed quietly, each lyric etched indelibly into his mind like markings on stone. "And I will never fade away," he reflected, inviting the final echoes of the tune to banish any lingering despair.

Then, as those last notes dissolved into the awakening air, James squared his shoulders and strode into the waiting world. There remained battles untold, demons yet to be vanquished, and injustices crying out to be righted. But in that shining, ephemeral moment, he allowed himself a breath—a moment to simply be.

He was alive. He was whole. His purpose shone like a guiding star, leading him through the uncertainties ahead.

For Sarah. For Wokingham. For the future they had fought so relentlessly to envision.

With a tranquil smile and eyes trained on the ascending sun, James continued down the serpentine road with a confident gait. Yet, as he pivoted away from the sanctity of the cemetery, a dark, ambiguous shape stretched across the horizon—a reminder that the rot might not have been vanquished, only transformed.

At that moment, his phone reverberated with an urgent chime —a notification flashing: "New Developments in The Circle

Investigation - Emergency Meeting Required." A surge of dread coursed through him. Despite the apparent triumph, the relentless corruption of The Circle seemed to be transmuting itself into novel forms, its ancient malice ever thwarted but never eradicated. Whispers of a deeper resurgence coiled in the back of his mind, suggesting that while one chapter had closed, the same shadowy specter of iniquity might have merely donned new guises.

Fierce resolve ignited within him. Though Wokingham's trials might have been superficially overcome, the battle against an enduring and ever-evolving evil was far from won. As he gazed at the fiery sky, James understood that his journey was entering an unforeseen labyrinth of challenges. The specter of corruption, ever elusive, loomed not as a vanquished foe but as a persistent, shifting presence—reminding him that sometimes the tide of darkness is not dispelled, only changed in form.

With that profound awareness fueling his determination and the strength of his allies lighting the path forward, James stepped resolutely into the new day, ready to face whatever threats might emerge next.

Printed in Dunstable, United Kingdom